IN YOUR DREAMS

#COLLEGE HUM♥R

PAUL BAUMAN

Rochester, New York

In Your Dreams #College Humor by Paul Bauman

Published by Flower City Press LLC, Rochester, NY 14609

Copyright © 2019 by Paul Bauman

Cover by Damonza

Printed in the United States of America

Paperback ISBN: 978-1-7325465-0-9
Ebook ISBN: 978-1-7325465-1-6

TITANIA

My Oberon, what visions have I seen!
Methought I was enamour'd of an ass.

OBERON

There lies your love.

TITANIA

How came these things to pass?
O, how mine eyes do loathe his visage now!

—William Shakespeare,
A Midsummer Night's Dream, Act IV, Scene I

ACT I

I fill out the last question of the exam and slap my pen on the desk with enough force to alert Professor Higgins. She swoops down the aisle from somewhere up in the rafters like a bird of prey and smiles at me while she collects my paper with her talons, both of us knowing full well that my math checks out. She preens at her business casual feathers, shrieks from her throat some type of hawk cry, and takes flight once more, to build a nest with the papers for all I care, because I'm out this bitch. Seventeen years of school are in the can, K through college, and you don't need to have a degree in finance to crunch those numbers. *Goodbye, Brockport. Hello, analyst position.*

I push open the door to the exam room never to return. Who's out in the hall to greet me but Alicia, my clingy stalker.

"Hi, Collin." She has red hair. "What's up?" She studies art. "Surprised to see me?" She's annoying.

"Surprised?" I repeat. "For my own well-being, I proba-bly should be."

She turns that answer over, but gives up halfway. "So, last exam. How does it feel?"

"Enchanting."

"You'll come and visit me next year, won't you?" She's a junior.

"It's kind of a long drive."

"You work twenty minutes away, and your parents live in Spencerport, one town over."

I ignore this, and she trails behind me as I walk through the valley of the shadowy hall.

"I expect many visits," she says. "Four visits per week. We're Facebook official."

I pause at the exit. "How?"

"You left your laptop open," she explains. "Teqnio. Never heard of that brand."

"It's imported." I blush. "How did you get in my house?"

"Carl let me in."

"That's normal."

"By the way, who is Stacey Greer?"

"An ex," I answer, confused. "Have you been checking my message history?"

"Maybe. Who's Vanessa Stockton?"

"A one-night stand from two years ago." I step out into the midday sun and breathe in the early summer.

Birds chirp. People chat. A train horn blares in the distance.

"Just one more." She pursues. "Jess Fisher."

I screw up my face. "Nobody."

"Nobody means somebody," she chimes.

"Nobody means nobody," I reiterate. "We don't talk about her." *It's far too embarrassing.* "Now, if you'll excuse me,

I've got some beers that need drinking. I think there's a party going on by the canal later."

"No drinking, you drunky! Tonight's movie night."

"Look, a) it's not working between us, b) I've just been relieved of two thousand tons of stress, and c) you'll understand next year."

"Or d) none of the above," she says. "Hey, where are you going?"

"Home to beat Carl's ass." I plod across the lawn at a healthy speed, then spot a bee and, deathly allergic, take off sprinting.

Evasive maneuver! Swat and run! Swat and run!

"Don't forget," she calls. "We're Facebook official!"

***

"That is an exceedingly incorrect statement," Carl surmises. "And unattractive. Grotesque even. It sullies my ears."

"What? Socializing *is* an important part of the college experience. Which, I might add, you just missed out on the last four years of." I block his view of the TV in his room. "I'm asking you to go to a party, dude. Not a funeral. The clock is ticking."

"Not interested." He waves me off and resumes Call of Duty. "It's Thursday and I have a lab at noon tomorrow."

"I have work at 9 a.m. and I'm going. Come on."

"Saying *come on* won't change my mind," he speaks as though he has a mouth full of marbles, "and I'm fairly positive you're only asking me because your friends all have exams."

"Come on. It'll be for two hours." I look around at his Periodic Table and StarCraft posters, realizing I have not

3

been in here in a while. "Plus"—I regain his attention—"you owe me."

"How so?" Carl pauses the game and folds his arms.

"Man, you let Alicia inside the house. This is sacred ground." I point down the hall. "She went on my account and changed my relationship status."

"Oh, I saw." He chuckles. "I gave it a like and wished you all the happiness in the world."

"It's not funny." I smack the controller off his lap. "You knew what you were doing and now I can't get rid of her."

"Like you could before," Carl retorts.

My face is steel.

"Fine." He shrugs. "It was rather uncouth. To make it up"—the words cause him physical pain—"I will cordially attend one outing." The knife's up to the hilt. "For two hours." The blade turns. "Where is it?"

"Awesome! It's on Erie Street." My phone rings in my pocket. "Some girl's 21st birthday party." Mom's calling. "I'll drive."

"Splendid." Carl coughs and holds out his hand. "My controller if you please, good sir."

I roll my eyes and hand him the baton. "We leave in thirty minutes. Get dressed."

"Is this a formal invite?" he yells down the hall.

"Yeah." I look back. "We got a pair of embossed cards in the mail, delivered by the Archduke of Wembley!"

I shut myself into my pigsty of a room. The rickety door sways back on its hinges, and I take the call.

"Get that piece of hybrid shit off the road, asshole!" the sound of my Dad's voice bellows alongside an air horn. He must be at work. He's a trucker. Mom's a nurse.

"Ricky, he's on." *Whoop, there she is.* Conference call. I bring the phone back to my ear.

"Hi, son," he says. "I-90 is fuckin' gonzo today!"

"Don't worry, Dad. Once I nail my interview, we'll be raking in more money than we'll know what to do with. That way you can stop picking up so many routes."

"Hey," he says. "I told you. It's you who's not to worry about us. Parenting works up-down, not down-up."

"Ooo," says Mom. "Your last final went well then, I take it?"

"No less than an A. I'm confident about that."

Mom comes up for air from her cigarette. "Excellent job."

"It was the class with the bird-faced lady, right?" Dad double checks.

"Ricky, be nice," she harangues him. "Look Collin, don't get hung up on this analyst position. If you set your expectations too high, you have that much further to fall."

"It's called climbing the corporate ladder, Mom."

I work in sales at Laissez-Fare. We're a payroll provider. I started part-time last semester on the internship program through school, and it's been so far so good.

"Until you fall off the corporate ladder and break your neck," Mom observes.

"I'm sure he's covered." I can hear the volume rise in Dad's voice. "The workers' comp taxes in New York State are up the ass!"

"Settle down, Ricky, you'll get a blood clot," says Mom. "Collin, I'm proud of you, dear, but if and when you get this salary job, I want you to save the money and build a life for yourself. I won't accept any of it."

"Mom, you guys—"

"Stop. Your father and I have discussed it. You're 22 years old. No one is taking you from us."

We've gone through this before. She thinks I want to provide for them because back when I was five and we were over in Astor Height Apartments, CPS came for me. Dad was too proud for welfare. Mom had a drinking problem. Food was scarce. Neighbors would call. It was a mess, and maybe it is related, but right as I'm about to rebut this point, Mom says, "Damn. I'm needed back in ICU. Congrats again, Collin. Don't party too hard."

"Drink a beer for me," says Dad. "Get off the road, you inbred twat goblins!"

~Conference Call Ended~

God, I love them. The analyst job is as good as mine, before they both work themselves into an early grave. I pocket my phone, close my laptop, and grab two Keystones out of the mini-fridge. Of course, every so often, you have to do you. I am my parents' son.

"Carl, it's time to start pregaming!"

"Nay, faith, let me not play a woman," I project my voice, positioned over the whopping Shakespeare book. "I have a beard coming." I rub my nonexistent whiskers and wait for Britney-Bear to say her line…and wait…and wait…and wait some more.

"Oh." Britney sits up. "You shall play it in a maaask," she announces all mellow and lackadaisical-like.

"Oh my God, Britney." I bury my head in the book. "You are the worst to study with."

"Why?"

I push my chair back from the kitchen table and point at the text. "You're missing lines."

She peers into the tome. "Oh. So I am." She leans back. "Hey, Jess."

"What?" I twist my hair around my fingers.

"If you're trying to become a kindergarten teacher, why do you have to learn Shakespeare? Kindergartners don't read Shakespeare."

I stop twirling and look at her, dumbstruck. "See, Britney. Now you're talking perfect sense."

"Genius status."

"But I still need to pass the exam or Grandma Fisher will do a backflip in her grave, rest her soul." I knock on the table.

*knock*knock*knock*

Those knocks came from the front door.

"Who could that be?" Britney strums her lip with her finger.

She follows me into the den and around the glass coffee table and, together, we climb onto the patent leather sofa to peer through the blinds.

knockknockknock

I can see a guy in a cut off tee and crop-cut hair banging on the door with his musclebound arm.

"I know you're in there, Blondie," he calls.

"It's Duncan," I whisper.

Britney tugs at her platinum blonde locks. "Is he talking to me?"

"No." We both have blonde hair.

"Oh." Britney turns her head, and a silver band of

light catches on her eyes, all noir style. "Should I call the authorities?"

"No." I hop off the sofa and stand by the door. "But be ready to."

"Roger that." Britney gets her phone out and looks through the blinds like an undercover fed.

I latch the chain and turn the knob, allowing my ex-boyfriend two inches of breathing room. In blows the piney scent of cologne that I had been so conditioned to in the beginning, which now only makes me sick. He pokes his nose into the crack to speak. He hasn't shaved in days.

"You're not going to undo the chain?" he asks, as the smell of mint gum drifts into my face. "Really?"

"No contact means no contact," I preach, wanting to slam his lips in the door.

"I know, I know." He bows his head. "Then I got to thinking." He swings up his chin. "It's your birthday tonight, and how could I have treated you so badly when your birthday was right around the corner? I thought I would show up here and take you out as a way of me saying sorry."

"Do you think I'm stupid?" I glance at Britney who solemnly shakes her head. "Why should it matter what day on the calendar it is for you to treat me right?"

"It shouldn't, I—"

"Did you notice, you didn't actually say *sorry*? You just phrased it funny as a way to skirt the issue."

"You know what I mean, Blondie."

"Stop calling me that."

"Fine, fine. How about this. If you're going out with a group of friends tonight, I join in and that way you can see how differently I act, and if you don't like what you see, I'll leave whenever you want."

"Like you would really leave on command," I say.

"I would."

"I'll pass." I start to shut the door.

He props it open with his foot. "If you're so against it, why are we still friends online?"

"It's called me being nice."

"Then why don't you play nice and tell me where you're going tonight?"

"I don't answer to you, but if I did, I would say I'm not going anywhere."

"You're Jess Fisher, and you're turning 21. Let's be real."

"I am real, and I have an exam at 11 a.m. The only man I'm spending time with tonight is named William."

"I'll kill him!"

I take a step back from this outburst. "Good luck. He's been dead 400 years, and if you ever come to my house again I'm calling the cops."

"What are they going to do?" Duncan balks.

"Not as much as my dad will."

At this new threat, Duncan removes his foot from the door. Dad is a big corporate exec downtown who dresses like a mob boss, and that whole persona combined with his domineering attitude seems to keep people in irons.

I get the door shut, slide the deadbolt, and release a long exhale. "Psycho."

"Total psychopath." Britney fixes the blinds and climbs off the sofa. "You should block him."

"I can't," I say. "He's got a nude photo of me. He'll make a Christmas card out of it and send it to my priest." Britney gives me a look. "It was from our early texting days. Stupid, right?"

"Live and learn," she says, understandingly.

"Thanks, Brit." I pull her in for a hug and peck her on the cheek.

"I know just the thing you need." Britney snaps her fingers. "Coffeeee."

"That would cheer me up." I pause. "I really shouldn't step away though. The exam…"

"I'll drive your car and you can bring the book to study on the way."

I worry Duncan might be camped out on the lawn, but then I hear the screech of tires and the fear quickly dissolves. Spurred on by his absence, Britney nods at me with eager eyes and a reassuring grin, the pros now weighted in her favor.

"Okay," I say. "Let me grab my things and check my blood sugar."

"Cool," she says. "You earned it, girl."

I go into the bathroom and check my levels. After a beep, the screen reads 101, which means no insulin. *Yay!*

Out in the kitchen, I stuff the big fat book into my pink backpack and shove off into the driveway where my Sunfire is parked. The colors of dusk reflect off the yellow gleam of the hood as the day turns into night. I toss Britney-Bear the keys, which she drops, but soon recovers, and we find ourselves cruising over the canal through town. She's gotten better at driving stick, so I crack the book and follow Helena, who follows Demetrius, into the Athenian Forest. When I look up, I expect to see a green two-tailed mermaid, but am instead greeted by a white shanty with a vacant drive and brown grass. *No, really, it's a straight hillbilly dwelling.*

"Um, Brit babe." I close the book. "Where are we?"

"The coffee is right in here." She opens the car door, grabs her purse, and wanders up to the strange house.

"Britney!"

She mounts the porch and disappears inside. Nervous, I take my bag with me, partly out of habit and partly to use as a weapon. The front door is left wide open. I call her name once but there's no answer. Walking back and forth on the footpath reveals nothing. The interior is in complete darkness no matter what angle I look at it from. The family who lives here are either out swimming in the canal or already have Britney tied up in their basement.

"Pssssssssst," says Britney from inside.

Drawn by curiosity, I totter onto the porch and into a dark front room. The lights flick on.

"SURPRIIIISE!" shouts an entire house-load of people.

Blood rushes to my face, and warm tingly feelings zap my body all over. The place is packed wall to wall, floor to ceiling, with friends old and new. Britney sheepishly waves with a tickle of fingers, and I can only choke on my emotion and smile. As the party transpires, I have just one drink, and another just one drink, and it's like I'm a frog who hopped into a warm pot of water that's slowly brought to a boil. It feels nice at first. Then you're dead.

ACT II

The ceiling fan greets me back to life in a blurry haze, circulating the odor of stale alcohol in my room. I can't tell if it's the room that's spinning or just my head or maybe only the fan or what, but in any event, I can get drunk again just by breathing in here, so that rules out any theories of me doing karate last night. However, no less than six concrete blocks were smashed over my head. *Yeah, six blocks feels right.* If I were to rank the discomfort from greatest pain to least, after the splitting headache comes the dry mouth, then the mysteriously sore hips, and lastly the blanket chafing my balls.

"Where time is?"

My nightstand clock reads 10:27 a.m., and I sound like a zombie, and I'm late for work! I leap out from under the covers in the direction of my pants and—

—I rattle awake to my left arm being yanked from its

socket. Something heavy just collapsed on the floor, and I think I felt something tear.

"Owww." I moan and wince and palm my shoulder, which is possibly dislocated. "That hurrrt."

Not only that, it feels like I got shot in the head with a beer can. I let out another moan while something sharp and hard cuts into my wrist. Wait a sec, this isn't my nice Egyptian down. This blanket is made of sandpaper! A sixty-watt bulb burns overhead, and a wad of rags over the window stops up all outdoor light. Skin itchy, hair in face, I dig my heels into the mattress and scoot crossways toward the side of the bed where my wrist is pulling me. That seems to decrease the pressure. What in God's name am I attached to?

It's a bracelet. *No. Holy shit.* I'm handcuffed! To another hand! Draped over the edge of the bed! Panicked and bruised, I fumble to my feet right when the owner of said hand tilts her head back and wipes away a mess of hair. It's a woman—*thank Christ*—and she squints at me, blonde and bleary-eyed.

"Jess?" My eyes go wide.

Hers must be adjusting, because she keeps looking at me upside down with her cheeks puffed out like an angry chipmunk. "Collin Marshall?" she says with outright disdain.

In a snap, she whips the comforter up to shield her face and boobs. "Not happening. Not happening. This didn't happen. I'm not here."

"I sure hope you are." Grinning, I grab a pillow and hold it between my legs in a Book of Genesis fashion. "You should feel honored."

"Oh my Gahd!" She waves our arms in a circle, inadvertently tossing a bra around that had slid from her arm down onto the chain. Furious, she heaves the covers off and peeks out to check, as if unsure of our predicament. "I'm fucking handcuffed!"

"I know!" I say, admiring the craftsmanship. "These things are legit."

Struggling with the cuff, she tries to push it over the bone of her thumb.

I find a tube of K-Y jelly on the nightstand and drop it next to her. "Here. Try this."

She glances at it, growls, then jams her thumb into the cuff even harder. When that fails, she goes back to waving her arm like a lunatic.

"Easy," I say. "My hand is attached to this thing."

She lets the cuffs hang midair between her left hand and my right, bra suspended, making some attempt to compose herself. "Where am I?"

"My house." I present the clutter and all its glory. "Fifty-four Gordon Street, Brockport, New York. Would you like the zip code too?"

I could smack him, but instead I sit up, distracted, and find myself studying his room like a curator would her first day on the job at a natural history museum, with first day jitters cranked to the max. Collin follows my eyes as they race from the spent Natty Ice cans on the windowsill to a pile of ratty work gloves on the dresser to a collection of SOLO cups leaning against a wall.

We move deeper into the drinking paraphernalia exhibit, my attention pausing on each item for .2 seconds before I realize it does not contain a Xanax, and I go zipping on to the next in a whirl. Dizzy bats/caveman clubs. *Nope.* Beer funnel with eight tubes/primitive watering can. *Nada.* Kanjam display/pair of cylindrical devices dating from the late Paleolithic whereby Aborigines would slap a piece of wafer-shaped neon plastic into a slot for ritual purposes not yet discovered. *No, no, no, and no.* Exiting drinking paraphernalia Xanax-less, I dash off to the exotic animal wing.

An old leopard-patterned vest hangs off a dusty flat screen, situated next to a fish tank with a cigarette butt floating on the surface. That poor goldfish, and *oh look*, he has a plaque—Mr. McGillicuddy—still alive, by some miracle.

Winding down, I gloss over the Fall Out Boy and Fetty Wap posters, all to arrive at a condom in the ashtray, the highlight of the tour. *Shit!* We definitely hooked up.

I can't stop smiling at the irony of it all. We met as freshmen in Music Listening class, a very important and life-changing elective. It was during the wind chime unit that she grabbed my attention. I developed a small crush, hardly noticeable, at which point I asked her out. Then, I got rejected for being too awesome for her. What other logical explanation could there've been?

He was a giant pussy. First I'm subjected to three months of furtive glances and awkward stares from the next row over.

Then when he did approach me, he stood there hemming and hawing like a gibberish-blundering weirdo. After a while he finally managed to formulate a coherent sentence and all that came out was, "Hey, you, uh, what, are, uh, you, uh, doing, uh tomorrow, uh, I gotta go." I didn't know how to let him down easy, so I just felt bad and said I had a boyfriend later online. I was young. I think it was during the finger cymbal unit. Who remembers with that bullshit class? I hope he didn't go back to his dorm after and make a shrine of me with pipe cleaners and crepe paper and weird shit. *Oh my God.* No one can know this happened! Why is he smiling? His smile is torture. He thinks he won something. I'll give him something to win.

"Wipe that stupid smirk off your face."

I smile brazenly, and that smile turns to a laugh. Four years ago I would've jumped at the chance to be with her. But now that I am a learned man, and know that her string of bad relationships and nightly bingers were red flags for crazy, I could care less.

Clenching her jaw, she looks at me with a crocodile glint in her eyes and balls up her fist. "You have thirty seconds to get the key."

"They're…not your handcuffs?"

"No, they're not mine." She bends her wrist to her chest, appalled. "You think I walk around with a bottle of 151 and a pair of handcuffs in my purse wherever I go?"

"I mean, if you're drinking that kind of firewater, yeah."

"It was my 21st birthday," she explains, pulling the bra under the comforter with her. "Still is."

"Um, happy birthday?" I let the pillow balance against my groin and spread my arms wide.

She scoffs and reels my hand behind her back to clasp the bra. "Where are my clothes?"

I spot a pair of panties near my foot and pick it up like a fish caught by the tail.

"That's not mine," says Jess. "Whose is that, your girlfriend's?"

I fling it past her head. "Define girlfriend."

"Define your face."

"Well, I'm told it's remarkably similar to Jude Law's."

Jess slaps at the bed, laughing nervously in that brassy way of hers. "On what fucking planet is this comparison being made?"

"Earth," I say, flatly.

"No. Just, no." Tears come to her eyes. "You actually kind of look like that one painting where that guy is clapping his face in a scream."

She's lying. I look like Jude Law.

Wait a sec. Jude Law? Britain. West End. Theatre. Globe. Shakespeare. My eyes dart to the nightstand clock. My hands begin to tremble uncontrollably. *Oh shit oh shit oh shit.*

"Oh shit!" A pang of terror recasts the lines in my face. "It's 10:30!? I have a final exam in half an hour!"

"A what?" asks Collin with a dopey expression.

I fidget to the edge of the bed, clinging to the sandpaper blanket. "A final!" I throw out my feet and push him aside.

"Skip it."

"Are you crazy!?" I stop halfway to my clothes by the door and let him have it. "Understand this. At 11 a.m. the LAST exam for my teaching degree will be handed out, and my ass will be in that seat to take it. I need to graduate on time. My future kindergartners need me to graduate on time. They need to learn, Collin! Do you want them setting off into the world not knowing their shapes? Not knowing how to count to 100! Not washing their hands after using the restroom! When they catch hepatitis, do you know who will be responsible?" I stab him with my finger. "You, Collin, you!"

"Well, this is quite the quagmire, I must say."

"You're goddamn right it is." Thinking he's on board, I wrap the blanket around me like a cloak and stoop to pick up my glitter-blasted denim. He lends me his arm, letting it trail from the floor to my waist as I crouch and rise to put on my jeans, affording me what privacy the situation allows. I do a little hop to get them over my hips and then turn to him.

"Why aren't you moving?" I shout. "Get your clothes on!"

He hitches a thumb toward the darkened window. "I have to get to work. I'm an hour and a half late."

I lose the blanket as the hairs rise on my arms and neck. *This is not fucking happening to me.* What the—How do I get him to—I feel the tears welling up.

"Please, Collin. Oh my God, I'll, I'll—"

She literally has nothing to offer me without making us feel cheap.

"I'll cry," she says defeated, and lowers her chin.

Yuck, melodrama. Must find hacksaw and cut loose girl. One thing's for certain. I need to bide for time. She can't go to work with me like this. Speaking of—

"Hold that thought," I tell her, digging into my jeans for my phone. "Why are my jeans wet?"

"You peed yourself," Jess appraises, "and need a diaper. If you don't come with me right now I'm telling everyone."

"Whatever." I unlock my phone, pillow held firm, and ignore a series of missed calls from Alicia in order to locate my work number. Scrolling through, I turn to Jess and reveal my priorities. "Let's deal with my life first before going anywhere near your dumpster fire."

Jess grits her teeth, and out comes her feisty side. "You have thirty seconds to get dressed, or I am dragging you to this exam whether you have clothes on or not!"

"Shhh." I shove the pillow in her face and bring the phone to my ear just as my boss answers. "Hey, Mike," I say with a sniffle. "I realize I'm late. I haven't had a chance to reach you. I've been at the hospital all morning."

Jess wrestles the pillow from me and bonks it between my legs.

"Olgh." *Balls!* "My grandma just passed."

The look on Jess's face is priceless.

"That's the third time you've used that excuse!" Mike shouts. "You have three grandmas?"

Oops. "Yeah. My stepmom's mom."

Jess sneers at me, her left arm dangling from my ear.

Mike was all corporate. "I've spoken with upper management, Marshall. They want me to let you go."

My landscaping gloves taunt me from the dresser with a demotion back to manual labor. "Please, Mike," I say. "I need this job. You know that analyst position just opened up. I took my last exam yesterday. My degree's official. Finance. I qualify."

"Listen closely, Marshall, and listen good. The only way I'm going against the top on this is if you send me a selfie with some old lady on a gurney, hooked up to a cardiogram, flatlining. And I want an obituary that reads 'survived by Collin Marshall' listing today as her date of death."

"Are you serious?" I pretend to sob. "This isn't a joke. My grandma died, man."

"And a picture of the tombstone," Mike tacked on.

"We're having her cremated."

"How many chromosomes do you think I'm missing, Marshall?"

"You have all 24 pairs, sir."

"It's 23."

"The more the merrier."

"Goodbye, Collin. You're fired."

~Laissez-Fare Mike Call Ended~

I read Collin's cell phone screen loud and clear and can't help a devilish grin. Dad is a senior executive there. *Gotcha now, bitch.*

"Fired?" I ask, unobtrusively.

"Yes. I am." Collin winces and lowers the phone in his fist. "Go ahead and gloat."

"Such a pity." I pretend to mourn and click my tongue. "Losing a nice cushy job like that."

"You don't get it." He's so cute, shaking in my web, totally helpless. "I *needed* that raise."

"And you had to go and lose it," I say. "What ever will you do?"

"Probably drive trucks for a living." He looks up, and I'm grinning like the damn Cheshire Cat. "Okay, have your laugh already."

"That's not why I'm smiling," I say. "You work at Laissez-Fare. So does my dad, who just so happens to be"—cue dramatic music, *dun-dun-dahhhhhn!*—"Mike's boss."

"No fucking way." Collin's eyes go buggy.

"Way."

"I'm inclined to believe you." Any last bit of skepticism melts out of his features. "Every hippie and their love child works there."

"You want your job back?" I narrow my eyes and ram my finger into his chest. "Get me into my exam. And Collin"—I get in his face—"so help me, if you tell *one* person in that office what happened last night, you can be sure the whole world will know it was nothing to write home about."

"Nobody writes home about that!"

"I should hope not." I pick some lint off my shoul-der. "The first act was rocky at best, and the ending had a weak climax."

Is she reviewing a Broadway musical? "Okay. I'll cooperate. I can't have these lies"—I give my spirit fingers a flitter—"circulating the airwaves."

"What lies?" Jess asks nonchalantly, testing out her rotator cuff like a baseball pitcher.

I grunt as our linked hands go round in a circle.

"Kidding." Jess stops the windmill. "Or am I?"

Muttering obscenities, I discard the pillow, pull up a dry pair of pants and loop my belt.

Now he obeys, and bonus points, my shoulder works. Isn't that the cherry on the cake?

"But for serious." I sigh out two lungfuls of air, mildly relieved, but still angsty AF. "Thank you."

"Got you, babe," says Collin.

"Don't call me that."

"First things first." He ignores me and reaches for a bottle of Pedialyte, then pops two Advils and washes them down. "Some of us try to plan ahead."

"Sure, Dad."

He extends the purple liquid to me.

"I'm not putting my mouth on that."

"Really?" He raises an eyebrow. "We just did way worse."

For the sake of dehydration, I begrudgingly palm the bottle and take a baby sip. "If I caught an STD, I'm sending your health insurance the bill."

"Um, pretty sure it doesn't work like a car accident," he says, notching his belt.

Wow. Brain fart. Where is my top? Torn to shreds on the floor. *Great.* I bend over and pick it up while he finishes gassing down the beverage for children.

I hold up my pink tank like a flag and can see the stitches have split apart from the armpit down to the hem.

"My shirt's ruined," I announce.

"Mine too." Collin has discarded the drink and has his blue tee spread out for inspection. "We're animals."

My God, we must've went HAM on each other, for reasons I'll never care to know or admit.

"What are we going to do?" I ask.

I can't wear one of his shirts. My left hand will never fit through a fresh sleeve. Not with him still attached to me. A new shirt would rip all over again. "Do you have duct tape? Or crazy glue? Clothespins, paper clips, sewing machine!"

"Yeah, in my back pocket for the fucking haberdashery I run on weekends." He holds out a finger to give pause, forming a pensive look in his eyes. "I've got it."

He dons his t-shirt like a poncho and leads me around the foot of the bed over a slew of dirty clothes and old food. *Jesus, Mary, hire a maid.* He snags the cords of a PS2 along our journey and sends it crashing to the floor. *Hire two maids.* I mean, this poor fish! I pick up the net and scoop out the cigarette butt while Collin rifles through a crate of school supplies in the corner. Butt retrieved, I set aside the net and stare in a fog at his stack of Blu-rays, waiting impatiently, when I detect an anomaly.

"Is that a VHS copy of *Spice World*?" I point.

"No!" He whirls around so fast, chucks the tape with his right hand, discs toppling, and proffers something shiny in his left. "Found the stapler!"

"Uhuh." Wetting the bed, no big deal. Guilty pleasure flick and he's red as a Gobstopper. "Let's go." *I'll blackmail this wannabe later.*

Jess hurries me into the hall, and all I can do is get my arm through my sleeve and hope she suffers from short term memory loss and chronic fits of dementia. The sound of wheels on hardwood emanates from Carl's room, who with a scoot from his computer chair soon materializes at his door, kicking back in his Spider-Man peejays.

"Collin, Alicia called. She says it's over."

"Good. Did she say why?"

Carl takes note of the handcuffs as Jess and I rush past. "Did she have to?"

"What are you, her secretary?"

"May as well be."

We get around the corner and shuffle down the stairs with relative ease.

"BLOW IT OUT YOUR ASS, CARL!" I holler up at him. Then I turn to Jess. "It appears I'm back on the market."

"Am I supposed to need this information?"

I spin around the kitchen in search of my shoes. "Yeah, tell your friends."

Who breaks up with a guy by calling his housemate? A brick through the bay window would have been less informal. Honestly, Alicia doesn't deserve another sober thought. It was a fun two weeks and that was that.

I scoop my Chucks up by the tongues while Jess slips into her pink uptowns. Footwear in hand, she prods me through the front door, into the rays of the blinding yellow Sunfire; a Pontiac Sunfire.

"Where's my Honda?" I strain my eyes like a photosensitive vampire.

"Who cares?" Jess frisks herself in a state of panic. "No no no no—What the cuck!" She jerks her head at me. "I don't have my keys!"

"Campus is a mile from here." I stop and listen. "You hear that droning sound?"

"It's a lawn mower. So what?"

Interest piqued, I descend the porch, Jess in tow, and stop in the yard to consider the car. Exhaust trails out by the back fender. The engine has been running this entire time. "Found the keys!"

Collin dances the jitterbug as I lead him around to the driver's side. Who knows with him anymore?

"Hot hot hot." He's barefoot on the blacktop.

I open the door and he herds me in. I'm about to object, but it makes more sense for him to drive. This way our outside hands stay free. I begin to crawl over the center console when he stops me in place.

"Hold up," he says, bearing the pain of the coals. "Let's ask a neighbor to borrow a hacksaw."

"Do they have one?" I pull him toward the car.

He doesn't budge. "I don't know."

"I thought you want to be an analyst."

"You're right. Too much risk." He steadies the cuffs on the roof. "Let's break them off in the car door."

"What!?" I wrench my hand in before he fractures it. "That won't work! Get in! Stop wasting time!"

"Fine!"

I climb over the E-brake while he weasels in and slams the door. He drops his shoes and stapler on the floor at my feet and puts his hands on the shifter. In one swift movement he grinds the hell out of my gears.

"God help me." I face-palm.

He woefully looks down at the knob, then up at me. "I can't drive stick."

Men.

Over the cupholders I go—cupholders filled with coffee, lip gloss, and pong balls. *Typical.* With my back to the windshield, I knock into the dream-catcher, and maneuver on top of Jess, placing my knee between her legs. Stuck in close quarters, she can only grimace at me while I smile back and drag my other foot over from the driver's side to the passenger's. Then my knee slips by accident and my head goes right into her breasts.

"Get off me, you big idiot."

"It wer an errsidert." I climb out of the melon patch and regain my footing.

"Sure it was." She shimmies out from under me.

I brace against the passenger window while she crab-walks onto her seat and settles in.

"Take two," she says.

Situated, I find my right hand sprawled uncomfortably across my stomach. At least the AC kept it cold in here for us. Jess plugs in the deck and EDM blares on the speakers. Instinctively, I cover my ears, but then she tugs my cuffed hand her way and I slap myself in the face.

"Ouch."

"What did you say?" She lowers the volume. "I need to see the clock." She hits the clutch, grabs the shifter, and floors it in reverse. With a squeal, the car barrels into the street, leaving tread marks and puddles of fluid in the driveway. My hand stretched to the wheel, she cranks it round to correct our course, and we're off.

Houses whoosh by too fast for my liking, which would explain the dream-catcher, put up in case her occupants fall asleep permanently. I pluck a bobby pin off the visor and wiggle it in the keyhole to busy myself. Maybe I can break free before she kills us. *Whoop, just ran a stop sign.*

We zoom over the mound of an intersection. 10:42 bounces on the dash, and my brain bounces in my skull. My parents better thank me for this. I've exposed myself to bodily harm so they can upgrade a tax bracket and be spared a pair of coronaries.

Thank God Jess didn't let me into her life back then. Her boyfriends don't run from crazy. They perish by it. What if we became a couple and I survived? In my delusional state, I'd have married this basket case. Can you imagine?

I recline in my La-Z-Boy, reading the daily periodical under my evening lamp when I hear a rappa-tap-tapping at the door. A key scratches around the lock from the outside as I flip to the Sports section with a slap of my hand against the print. The wife has decided to turn the key right-side up, a habitual practice, and the scratching continues. I think she's made entry but she rappa-tappas again. In a moment the sliding window opens above the sink, and I hear a flower pot go down.

The faucet turns on as she struggles to hurdle the window, majestically followed by a thud on the linoleum floor.

"Fickle fuck," she mumbles.

I lick my mustache, lower my reading glasses to the tip of my nose, and pan across our apartment, furnished like the set of *Leave it to Beaver*, because she spent all of our savings on booze and we've been reduced to thrift store knick-knacks. In the corner of the set, a silhouette teeters in the doorway, illuminated by the faint glow of my evening lamp, hanging on a chain, above my chair, which I use to see. Smeared lipstick, a bedraggled weave, and sliced jeans belittle her presence. Without fail, a handle of Captain Morgan is anchored at her side.

I fold the paper down. "Cheat on me yet?"

"No-wo."

"Congratulations." I rustle to Business. "Our marriage lives to fight another day. Now go read our daughter, Kahlúa, her bedtime story."

Mrs. Marshall nods affirmatively and staggers down the hallway, swiping picture frames off their hooks like a drunken rhino. Panes crackle as they hit the shag carpet, and by some coordination of hand, eye, and nose, she makes it into Kahlúa's bedroom.

"Mommy, you smell like a licorice scented marker."

"That's just adult smell," says Mrs. Marshall. "Where were we? Once upon a time," she begins. "There was a pirate named Captain Henry Morgan. And in one six seven four A.D. he was knighted by the King of England. And Sir Captain Mo wanted to be gervner of Jamaica. And you know what? He did became gervner. And everything was irie. Ya mon. Right by duh beach."

Is she reading from the back of the liquor bottle?

"Mommy, you scare me."

I drop the paper on the side table, march down the hall, and, with no great surprise, see Mrs. Marshall out cold on Kahlúa's bed.

"Shhhh, Daddy. Mommy's sleeping."

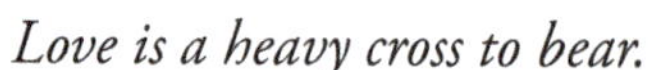

Love is a heavy cross to bear.

I lay on the horn as I cross over the double yellow in order to pass a Buick before an oncoming Jeep has a chance to blast us into oblivion. Now all three of our vehicles honk as I white knuckle the wheel and tear in front of the Buick, my rear end veering into a fish tail.

"Not trying to die today," says Collin, un-bunching his panties.

"Sorry." I downshift, and we rumble around a 90 degree turn onto Main Street. "We have to think of a way to get you into the exam."

"Um." He crams his foot into his shoe one-handed. "Walk in."

"And the excuse as to why we're handcuffed?"

I lift my arm so he can align the sequins on my tank top in the jaws of the stapler and suture me up.

"Tell your professor you handcuffed us." He squeezes out a staple.

"Are you for real?" *SMH.*

"How else did we get like this?"

Oh my Gawd. Did I cuff us? It's bad enough as it is. If I'm the one who handcuffed us, I'd like, slit my wrists five minutes ago.

"There is zero chance that happened," I assert, "and solving that mystery is last on our to-do list."

"Then tell your professor you don't know. Tell them the truth."

"Like you told your boss the truth?"

"I'm turning over a new leaf, starting now."

"You don't understand." I put my knees on the wheel. "I can't have a scandal. Walluski is a hard-ass. If I show up like this, he'll retract his letter of recommendation from the elementary school I want to work at." I lift an old Starbucks cup from the holder and tilt the lid to my nose.

Collin puts his hand on the wheel and I swat him away.

"I'm driving here," I tell him. "You're supposed to think."

He sets to work stapling his own shirt. "Say we're conjoined twins."

"Then where were you the whole semester?"

"The doctor sewed us back together. You were lonely."

I crack a smile. "He is educated."

Collin twists his neck around to look at something out of the back windshield.

"What do you see?" I ask, watching a turn coming up.

"Blue lights."

"Ambulance," I reply, and unconcerned, I spin the wheel.

We pull onto Monroe Avenue, a street running parallel with campus where expansive lawns and boxy buildings unravel out the back window. I don't see any cops on our tail, so I face front, where a pair of heart-shaped sunglasses dangle down from the visor. Mesmerized, I find myself staring at my own reflection. Suddenly, inspiration hits and I grab the steering wheel as she's about to turn into Lot F.

"Hands off, grabby."

"Stay straight and park in Lot A," I say. "I have an idea."

"An idea that involves driving away from the lecture hall? My exam is back there."

"There's a blind guy I know who hangs out in Harrison."

"The guy who calls everyone either Big Poppa or Foxy Lady?"

"Yeah, that's him. Blind Frank. We're going to borrow his glasses and cane. I'm your new disabled brother."

She shakes her head in astonishment. "I am so fucked." But, out of options, she reluctantly agrees.

We cruise past the academic halls, nearing the opposite edge of campus when the engine sputters. Jess uses her coasting power to pull onto the grass in front of Lot C where the car gives one final jolt and stops. I don't know how she wound up in this clunker. I'm just glad she's not whippin' a Maserati through this one horse town.

The asphalt field that is Lot A is off in the distance, but, as luck would have it, Harrison Hall, our target destination, is directly behind this towering dorm across the street.

"Shit." Jess surveys the area. "I'm going to get a ticket here."

"You're right. We should wait obediently for the cops to show up."

"Funny." She sneers.

The clock on the dash reads 10:53 when Jess pulls the key from the ignition. She gets out, and I climb over the gearshift, a feat which I somehow duplicate, tobogganing headfirst through the chute, nearly kicking the rearview mirror clean off in the process.

Jess helps me up, sniffing at her armpit. "How do I smell?"

I rise to the stench of burning rubber and press my nose to her top to investigate. "Like you went to an AA meeting held at a liquor store."

"No bueno." She draws me into a stoop and folds down her seat.

Out comes a pink backpack, one of those old L.L. Bean ones with your initials on it. I haven't seen them since like 4th grade. She unzips the JKF bag, and removes a bottle of wine and a red book with Shakespeare on the cover. She sets them both aside, and I have no comment, but when she uncaps a bottle of perfume and starts spraying me down with Eau de Stripper, I do have a comment.

"Do you feel better now?" I spit out the mist, my face a lemon.

"Much," she says, too proud of herself.

"I'm glad." I toss the perfume in the car and shut the door. "The backpack we can use."

We plunge our linked hands into the bag and take off

running into the street. Tires skid and a horn beeps as we're almost clipped by a passing Smart Car.

"Holy feces!"

I'll drop kick that thing, and I try to, but Jess pulls me off and urges me forward. So, ignoring the clown in the glorified golf cart, we skirt around the 12-story dorm with my shoelaces thwacking at my ankles, over the grass, and onto the sidewalk leading to Harrison, a squat dining hall flanked by some dorms. Inside, I scan the entryway for my middle-aged buddy, Blind Frank. I have no clue if he attends classes here, or is affiliated with the college in any way, shape, or form. I honestly think he just comes for the pasta.

He's one of those people you can go months without speaking to and pick up like nothing's changed. We constantly rip on each other and *blah blah blah*. There's no sign of him by the lunch counter. Jess pivots her head this way and that, looking unnerved and approaching unhinged. There's no sign of him anywhere. I lead Jess around a corner into a niche seating area with café tables and, *thank the Lord*, we bump right into him.

"I smell burrito farts," Frank announces. "That you, Collin?"

"Yes, it's me! Frank, listen, I need to—"

"What's up, Big Poppa?" He extends his hand to Jess and there it lingers. "Why you smell like a lady, Coll?" He takes an audible whiff. "You shopping at Vicky Secret's again?"

"Listen." I take Frank's hand, slapping him up. "I need to borrow your glasses and cane."

"Sure, you can borrow my glasses and cane." Frank pauses. "Got any weed?"

"Uh." I check my pockets while Bob Marley stares up at me from Frank's t-shirt with a look of Rastafarian bliss.

Okay, enough pussyfooting. "Please, Frank, my name is Jess. It would save my life. You have no idea. I have an exam in, what time is it? Like now."

"Jess? Not the Unconquerable Jess Fisher?"

"The what?" I ask, in a WTF tone.

"Oh, uh, he means it as a compliment," says Collin, scrambling, "like, uh, the Unsinkable Molly Brown."

"Right, Molly Brown." Frank straightens his vest and points. "Ten-four."

"I'm flattered." *So this is how the proletariat sees me.*

"Frank, it's just for two hours." Collin places a hand on his shoulder and Frank, stupefied, looks in the opposite direction. "I'll explain later. You know I don't have any weed."

Frank begins to hand over his possessions, but then hesitates. "Will you take me to lunch one day? I rarely find friends to eat with," he says with a frown.

"Yes, Frank, lunch. We'll go to Red Robin and shit our pants after. We're in a hurry here."

"Three times," says Frank.

"That's pushing it," Collin backpedals.

Is this my life? This is my life. It's not my life. I am inside an illusion. With a blind guy and a jackass. I pinch myself. *Shit, no I'm not. I'm IRL.*

"Collin!" I stamp my foot. "Take him three times!"

"What am I, made of money?" I ask. "We split it." "Done," says Jess.

"Great, it's settled," says Frank. "Now what about collateral?" *Always the hard negotiator.*

I reach for the initial bag and fork it over. "Here."

"Wait, I need my pencil for the test." Jess unzips a compartment and removes a wild pencil with an oversized eraser head. I think it's some type of gay pride unicorn.

"It's Rainbow Dash." She waves the pencil at me like a fairy godmother. "She brings me good luck on exams."

"Well princess," I say, playfully, "we're gonna need it."

"Uh, this isn't a pink backpack, is it?" asks Frank.

"No, no, it's black. She's emo."

"Good." He shakes the bag by the strap at each syllable. "Cuz I don't wanna look like no humpstick walkin' down no hallway with no pink backpack! Mm-mmmm." He shakes his head. "Hell naw!"

"Frank, it's not pink," says Collin. "Just give me your stuff."

"Yeah, Big Poppa, I hear ya." Finally, Frank parts with his peppermint cane and John Lennon sunglasses, whereby Jess and I book it for the front exit.

We burst onto the courtyard scene, sun blinding and people everywhere. This is Brockport on exam week, a hive buzzing with plaid-shirted jabronis and basic girls for days. You know the types. The guys who bark without bite, Addied out of their minds 24-5. The women who follow the herd, lost in the blur of trends and celebrities. They run amok, hands firmly clamped to their hot PSLs or whatever basic themed drink the nearest holiday mandates them to purchase. Easter was basically two weeks ago, so I bet the lattes are Peeps flavored.

It's these types Jess and I race to outmaneuver like pegs

on a Plinko board, dodging the occasional glances from our fellow jabronis and basics alike—yes, Jess and I make the cut. I mean, come on. Look at us.

FML. People are going to recognize me. This is so embarrassing. I can feel a tear in my social fabric with every foot gained in our race through the crowd, a fabric which took so long to sew, thanks to my social networks, platforms, and butterflies, weaving my rep with meticulous care soon to be shredded like the side of my shirt. The stitches, hopelessly, are unbounding, but what else can I do? I press on, blowing a bee out of my face as I charge between two sophomores.

Bee-EE-ee-EE-ees.

Collin's shoelaces almost face-plant him as he spins back and forth in a half-circle swinging that stick around like a child set loose on a piñata. We loiter by the giant red phallic statue among the flowering rhododendrons, brought to a grinding halt.

"The bees!" he shouts. "The bees!"

"Collin, my final." I tug at his shirt, ducking the cane. "We can play with the bees later."

He runs around like a wild man while I try to keep up.

"I'm allergic," he says, out of breath.

I had this same problem with the kids at recess during student teaching. "You have to be still and they won't bother you." *Of course, should that fail for the kids, I did have their EpiPens handy.*

"They're in attack formation!" He jerks left to right doing some hardcore swashbuckling.

"Guess you don't want your job then."

Braving the bees, re-incentivized, I stand erect with my cane out and joust our way toward freedom. Jess hurries alongside me, her top sparkling in the light; a jogging flame. We avoid a squadron of jabronis, and some basic girl comes prancing right for us! I juke left. Jess swerves right. But it's no use. The girl bellies into our cuffs and her drink goes flying everywhere, all with her phone call so rudely interrupted. Baffled, she looks at her spilled drink, then at the cuffs, then at Jess, then at me, then her phone, then Jess again, then back at the puddle.

"We escaped from prison," I tell her.

"We're rehearsing a play," says Jess.

"We're rehearsing a play where we escaped from prison," I amend.

No time for this basic nonsense, we hightail it out of there.

Oh Gawd. I hope that girl didn't recognize me from psych class. I replay the scene in my head to make sure, but as we come up on Edwards Hall, she's brushed to the wayside. Urgently, I take the lead and scurry up the stairs while the shackles rattle in tempo with my feet. At the top, we hurl open the door and dash inside. The sun shines through the glass façade which lines the hallway, which in turn wraps the entirety of the lecture halls within.

"Did you see those bees?" asks Collin, still winded.

"Um, yeah." My voice carries. "They're just bees."

"Just bees?" He talks with his hands. "Those are 10-millimeter-long floating darts loaded with a deadly venom that can kill you!"

Why, why, why did I have to drink so much? Being 21 feels exactly the same as it must have when Prohibition ended. Once you're legally allowed to drink it's like, been there, done that.

"Okay," I say, carrying the team, "let's keep calm and you know the drill."

He nods compliantly. "What room is it?"

"Number 105. Right here." I park us before the door. "Tie your shoes."

I bend over so he can lace up.

"Phones," he warns.

"About that. Mine's MIA."

"That's surprising." He smirks. "I remember you staying strapped to your phone like a terrorist to a timebomb."

"Left it in my other vest." I dive into his pocket and set his phone to silent. "Get into character."

He puts on the shades and—

"Jesus Christ Almighty! These things are prescription." I hold them up to the lights. "I can't see through these."

"It's okay." Jess guides the glasses back to my nose. "I'm helping you anyway."

She grabs my wrist and I can tell she's been crying sweat.

"Are you nervous?" I ask.

"A little." Her voice comes out small.

"We'll do fine," I hope, digging for resolve, something to restore confidence in my plan.

"You'll be at your desk Monday morning," she says, encouragingly.

Side by side we stand, I on the left, she on the right. I grip the candy cane in my left hand as Jess lifts up my shirt and stashes my right hand against the small of my back, my arm bent, knuckle to spine. And that is where we hide this shiny elephant. A little crude, but it will have to do.

"Everyone good?" she asks. *Who's everyone?* "Good." I swear she just kissed that unicorn. "Here goes our futures."

It's deep breath in, deep breath out, and in we go. She leads me through the drafty threshold and into the lecture hall. Through my periphery, I can barely make out the lay of the room, and it strains my eyes to look. Behind us, the latch of the door clicks into place, sounding like a pin drop in a pool of silence. Rows of chairs squeak at the intrusion, though I doubt anyone takes notice. They're just anxious for the exam.

OMG. Every single person here is staring right at us. My feet scuff across the carpet making small advance, and it feels as though we've stepped onto a stage without so much as a read-through. Walluski commands the head of the class looking very professorial in his tweed jacket, combover do, and no-nonsense demeanor.

"Very good, Miss Fisher, one minute to spare," he booms, "but your friend will have to wait outside."

"Please, Professor Walluski," I begin, "I had to pick my brother up from therapy and have nowhere else to take him. He's extremely dependent and can't be left alone. You see, every morning I have to remind him that he looks like Jude Law so he doesn't get self-conscious and harm himself."

That is a gross mishandling of facts.

"What a heavy burden for you," Walluski concedes, albeit condescendingly. "He only bears a slight resemblance."

I told you! Wait, only slight?

"He does?" I scrutinize his face with the rest of my class, as if seeing it for the first time. *Maybe I was too harsh.* "I do see it now." I turn his chin. "Such a precious snowflake he is."

I'm going to kill her. It's been decided.

"Be that as it may, Miss Fisher," says Walluski, "Mister McAdams is also blind, and he manages day-to-day activities with little aid."

Oh great, didn't see that coming.

Shoot, I forgot about him.

What's his exam, in braille?

He must be taking his test in another room as we speak.

Better think fast, Jess. I like my job.

Think think think, stupid brain.

We're fucketh'd.

Bingo!
"My brother is also a deaf-mute, sir. He has trouble putting his own pants on. I try and I try to reason with him, but my instructions never sink in."

"I can see that," Walluski agrees. "His fly's undone."

This is a trick. I can't flinch. I can't move. I hear nothing. He wants me to look down. Wait for it…*Whoa.* I feel a sudden pressure on my jeans. Jess is zipping me up. My fly really was undone!

"There. All fixed." He's probably glowing on the inside over that one. *Please, for the love of God, just don't pop a boner, Collin.*

Nice save, Jess.

I think we're in the clear, but then a random student begins mouthing off from the back of class. His voice is snively and I want to punch it—

"How does he know what Jude Law looks like?"

Shut up, Derek!

"He doesn't," I say. "He just equates Jude Law with being dapper and sexy."

I coil my finger around Collin's hair for added effect.

"Okay, Miss Fisher." Walluski's had enough. "Bring your sibling down. Down here in front, where I can make sure that no cheating's going on."

"Thank you, thank you, thank you so much, sir!"

Jess nudges me to move. The floor declines into a slope. In a matter of paces, I put my foot out like normal, but miss the carpet and keep falling. Quickly, I catch myself. The stumble is momentary, though enough to arouse Walluski's attention.

"Perhaps you would like to utilize the ramp entrance leading in from the hall?"

"It's okay, thanks." Jess wrangles me down the next step. "I'm teaching him stairs."

I almost take another spill so decide to use the cane, smacking it between the wall and the desks, nearly bopping students in the head, judging by their sour reactions.

I smile and cringe, whispering a sorry here and there while trying to assist my buffoonish brother down the aisle. I slap his arm to get him to stop waving that cane around, but to no avail. He spears the handles of a purse and knocks it into our path. I whisper another sorry and press my hand to his gut, accidentally jabbing him with my pencil as I help steady him.

Upon reaching the bottom, we carefully slink into the front row, alongside a desk that spans the width of the room. Once in the center, we creep to a halt, where I tug on his shirt so that we can sit simultaneously. *Phew. Made it.* I can't collapse the cane without using both hands, so we let it lie on the desk.
Laughter echoes in the peanut gallery, and I hope to God they're not laughing at me.

"Hey, up in back!" Walluski calls. "Laugh again and you get an F."

A stack of papers spanks the desk before us, and I try not to jump.

"Here's your booklet, Miss Fisher. Phones off, people! Belongings on the floor!" Walluski lowers his voice and speaks to Jess with an edge. "Beverages included."

Oh no. He's still sore about the time I spilt coffee on his favorite tie. I hope he grades leniently.

"No one is to leave until all booklets have been collected! THE EXAM BEGINS NOW!"

I flip over my sheet and am greeted by three lines of text:

Apply an '-ism' to any of the plays we read this semester in the form of a 5-page essay. I want a compelling argument and an imaginative title.

GTFO, *I'm* not Shakespeare! Okay, think Jess, think. For the play, I should definitely go with *A Midnight Summer's Dream*, since that's the one freshest on my mind. Or was that *A Midsummer Night's Dream*? Dang it! I always mix that up. Okay, no need to freak. We'll get back to that. What about the -ism? I glance around the room as if the answer is written somewhere on the blackboard. When I realize that it's not, my eyes drift to Collin, sitting there without a care in the world.

Douchebag-ism.

Now wait a minute. How can you split going to three lunches between two people? One and a half for me? One and a half for Jess? We'll have to share a time slot with Frank. Did she sneak a date in there? I better ask her to clarify. I had a crush on her, I admit, from a long time ago when I was eighteen, but enough gushing. It may've been a hallucination, and our current arrangement is strictly business.

That is, unless, *unless*, by some token intervention, divine or medical, she's changed. *Yeah, right.* However, there is a possibility that she doesn't let men treat her like garbage anymore, that she got a clue and cleaned up her act. I'll have to get to the bottom of this. Who pursues the chase after the catch? Drunk people. That's who.

Okay, recap. Puck runs around the forest handing out jungle juice. Titania, the fairy queen, is obsessed with kids. Then, all of a sudden, she gets hammered and wakes up handcuffed to a man-child. *Er, right.* I mean man-donkey. And Titania's obsessed with an Indian changeling boy. And Puck doled out flower juice. *Wow, where is my head?*

No wait. Maybe I'm onto something. Collin the sales rep here is a lot like Nick Bottom, the weaver, as they both have donkey heads. Also, they're both working class and have no mobility, or nobility, inside the city of Athens anyway. But in the forest they're allowed to mingle with the royalty of Titania. The rules are stripped, among other things, and it becomes anarchy. *Anarchism!* Versus, what? The rigid social structure of Athens, which is…casteism. How do you pronounce that? Who gives a shit? There's my essay. Excitedly, I lay pencil to paper for my title:

The Clash of Bottom and Titania:
When Blue-Collar meets Blue-Blooded

Why is she moving around so much? She's going to give us away. Oh, don't tell me. She's left-handed, and she keeps trying to write with it. Like one in every thousand people are left-handed, and I had to go and get tethered to one of them. Gratefully, the cuffs are still behind my back and out of sight. In the refuge of my shirt, I close my hand over hers to give her a hint, but it's too late. Loafers edge into view past my nose—brown suede with a gold buckle. I can feel Walluski's presence, and, based on how his shoes are poised, he probably has his arms crossed.

Walluski has a fist on his hip, searching the area for tom-foolery. I squeeze Collin's hand, hidden under cover, and feel the sweat pooling in the cups of our palms. Playing it cool, I continue to scribble with my right hand, even though my cursive comes out worse than a kindergartner's. It's not my fault I wasn't born ambidextrous.

To say that keeping six of our limbs calm and loose while our hands remain clasped together by early onset rigor mortis is nerve-wracking as hell would be an understatement. Walluski is not making it easy. He just stands there, ticking his nails on the desk. C'mon leave! Nothing to see here! Move it along! Why aren't you leaving!

After an eternity—I'll kiss that silly unicorn it's been so long—Walluski shifts his weight, splutters into his lips, and finally migrates elsewhere.

Crisis averted, Jess lets her hand go limp.

I don't know what that was I felt. Fear certainly, but something more. An odd sense of protection. From Collin? I glance at him. He's ambitious, I'll give him that, but to think for one godly instant he can make me feel protected would be plain spoony. I glance again. Maybe he has changed. Though, what if he hasn't? What if he's a complete doormat who lets women walk all over him? Dare I dream?

I come home from working a double to a sink full of dirty dishes, a pot of chicken noodle soup boiling over, and Jess Junior eating a tub of Mint-Ting-A-Ling off the kitchen floor.

"Collin, what the actual fuck!" I call up the stairs, setting down my school bag and waitressing apron.

He's nowhere in sight. Appalled, I scoop our daughter up, get the stove, and have Jess Junior rubbing her palms back and forth under the tap by the time Collin decides to make an appearance.

"Hello, Jessica, my love, my treasure, my sweet."

"Collin, why was our two-year-old daughter left unattended eating half a gallon of ice cream off the kitchen floor?"

"She asked me for it."

"She's lactose intolerant! I can already smell it in her onesie."

"I forgot, my peach, my pie, my peaseblossom." He dives at the ground and envelopes my legs. "Please, oh please, oh please forgive me."

I roll my eyes in disgust. "Just be more careful." I shake him off. "What have you been doing?"

"Making phone calls. And I have not one, but two tasty morsels of news!"

"Jesus, Mary, what are they?" I carry Jess Junior straight to the toilet where I hold her above the seat, poor thing.

Collin follows me in and stops at the door to reveal his news. "Today I quit my job as an Elvis impersonator so we can spend every second of every minute of every day together, my pear, my plum, my porridge."

Oh dear Gawd, my father was right. He *is* a pussy.

"And when we approach old age," Collin goes on. "I'm picturing a homicide-suicide scenario. This way neither one of us will have to outlive the other. Oh, it'll be swell. Then afterward, I'm thinking we can be interred in the same coffin, which brings me to my second tidbit. I bought a plot this morning at Holy Sepulchre, so we're all squared away on the cemetery front. Totally squaresy. The lady on the phone thought it was a little weird, but she said she can swing it."

I cringe hard and feel my muscular system wanting to abandon my skin where it stands and run for the hills and dales.

"I told you I'd start contributing to this family, or my name isn't Mr. Collin Fisher."

"How about I shoot you and nobody shoots me?" I propose, wincing from the odor.

"Semantics, shmemantics." Collin bandies his hand about. "We'll iron out the details later."

"It has just occurred to me." I rise with JJ. "I am an irreversibly raging lesbian."

The scary part is, Collin's probably over there thinking about me right now.

I wonder where my car went. Wrapped around a tree somewhere? *Eh, I'll figure it out.*

Okay, maybe that whole pushover mentality doesn't jive with how he's acted so far. I'll grant him that. But, hmmmm, you think he really has changed? That feeling I got from him was totally   unexpected. I've got to know what it was, and I shall employ every trick in the book to find out.

By all means, let's go already. Collect your exams, Walluski. I have to drain the lizard. He just picked up Jess's booklet, and after another, less excruciating eternity, I believe he has them all.

Nope, there's one test left. I push Collin back down and steal a glance over my shoulder. Walluski, arms folded, towers over the last student waiting for him to finish.

Hurry up, Derek! People have shit to do!

The breathing, coughing, and tapping among the rows adds a layer of white noise to the room, ample proof that everyone's going stir crazy.

Derek barely gets his last i dotted when Walluski snatches the pencil from his hand and his paper out from under him.

"Okay, everyone can go!" says Walluski. "Have a good summer. And a good midsummer! And even a good late-summer. Adieu!"

Kill me now. Jess pinches me to stand, and up I get. Heading the opposite way we came in, I take the lead and bang my thigh into each and every chair that crosses my path. Thankfully, the clatter is drowned out by the lingering well-wishes and abrupt departures of the other students. Not so thankfully, I'm bruised, and funnel into the aisle where Jess do-si-dos around me to guide my ascent, right when a chubby voice calls out, "Hey Helen, nice shades."

Who said that? I'm deaf. I'm deaf. If Walluski wasn't around, I'd beat that jabroni with my cane.

Jess has me lower the weapon, and, resuming character, I transmit a Morse Code of wandering clacks, on a quest for solid ground.

clickclickclick*click*clickclick

"Shit," Walluski mutters from the podium.

He saw the cuffs. He must have. I slow my walk practically to a standstill, bow my head, and listen.

"We're short six pencils," he grumbles.

Jesus! I resume my stride and feel a blast of warm air. We've left the lecture hall.

"Keep your glasses on," says Jess.

She escorts me through the exit to the courtyard, down the steps, and we're out of there.

"Oh my God." I put as much distance between us and the exam as I possibly can. "My heart is racing."

And the heat is relentless. Collin is already airing out his collar. "Did you hear what that guy said?" He removes the shades, blinking repeatedly in the bright sun.

"Yeah, he was a jerk." I erase the thought with my pencil. "Listen, thanks for sitting through that with me and coming up with that crazy idea."

"Job aside, I couldn't let you fail."

I run my fingers through my hair. "I can't believe it worked. I am so glad he bought that."

"Putty in our hands," he says. "How'd you do?"

"Eh." I make a so-so gesture. "I got tripped up a little at first, but lucky for me, I am the queen of BS-ing finals."

"It was all the unicorn, I'm sure," he says, pointing to the other end of the courtyard. "Come on. Frank's probably lost."

We blend in with the crowd, so happy with our success that I'm overflowed with joy. On top of that, Collin's being nice to me in a non-creepy, non-douchey way. Who would have thunk?

We navigate our way back to Harrison where we find Frank stumbling the first floor, triple checking to make sure the wall in front of him hasn't teleported into another dimension.

"Frank!" I call.

He turns to confront me. "I'm high, I'm blind, and you people gave me a pink backpack!" He shakes the bag in his fist. "Do you have any idea what that does to my image?"

"No." Jess twirls her pencil at him. "I think that color looks hot on you, Frank."

Frank raises the bag level with his wonky eyes, shows it off, and grins. "Ya think?"

"Yeah man," I say, "it's a good look."

"Yeah, well, it's still pink, and now it's four lunches." Frank trades in the bag.

"It's three, Frank." I hand him the shades. "You gave me prescription lenses. I couldn't see shit."

Frank pushes them up the bridge of his nose. "Welcome to my world, baby."

"Who told you the bag was pink anyway?" I ask.

"JKF's home-girl, Britney. She came over talking 'bout lost keys and black-outs and sayin' sorry and how it was all meant to be a joke, but it went too far."

"Oh." I wheel around to face Jess. "So, your friend is the one who did this?" No response. "Jess?"

I am not Jess. My name is Titania, and I am a goddess, and I live by a bank where the wild thyme blows.

She stands there silent with her cheeks turning a deep red hue. I don't know who Britney is, but she definitely knows who I am, clearly through Jess talking about that creeper, aka me, who asked her out in Music Listening class four years ago. Britney, I'm telling you it was super weird. Yeah, the didgeridoo unit. I don't care who he looks like. Such a creeper. Latte cheers. *clink* What can you say? Girls talk. Well, not right this minute, anyway. Jess is still a mute tomato.

Bacardi. Forest. Birthday. Oberon. Exam. Must. Kill. Britney.

"And you thought I cuffed us," I tease her. "In your dreams."

Are you sure that we are awake?

"Cuffed *what?*" asks Frank.

"Jess and I woke up this morning in real-life working handcuffs."

"Wooo, baby!" Frank nods approvingly. "Better her than a dead hooker. Then you really got problems." He adjusts his frames. "Well, the art department's prolly got a chainsaw or chisel or whatnot, and you know where to find me for lunch.

Now, if y'all excuse me, I've got pressing engagements ta tend to. Ciao, suckas."

He chucks up the deuces and I watch him saunter away, genuinely happy for the assist.

"They let him operate a chainsaw?" I ask.

Jess pats at her face, no longer catatonic. "We'll ask him over lunch." She looks up at me and flips the hair from her eyes. "Jude."

"Lunch?" My stomach rumbles as the aroma of pasta sauce drifts out of the kitchen and up my nostrils.

"We split one, remember?" asks Jess. "It's only fair."

"True." So she did notice the lunch thing.

"Art room?" She tilts her head to the courtyard exit.

I feel the weight of my bladder against my groin and croak out, "Bathroom."

"Absolutely not." She bops me with her wand. "You go. I'll wait here."

ACT III

He swats at my hand in a delayed reaction. Then, legs crossed to stave off the flow, he says, "I promise I won't make it any more awkward than it needs to be."

I look at him like he's got snakes for hair.

"I'm not asking you to hold it for me," he clarifies.

"I've seen it once," I say, deflated, "I suppose I've seen it a hundred times."

"Atta girl."

I elbow him in the gut. "Do I get a salt lick?"

He cups his palm to my mouth, which I smack away in playful protest. With Rainbow Dash back home, we zip up the bag, now guarding our hands, and take a heightened walk to the opposite end of Harrison. Here in the entryway, I push open the door to the women's room, and that's when Collin jerks back the reins.

"Whoa," he says, "No harassment charges for me today, thanks."

"And me standing in the men's room is somehow better?"

"Yeah," he says. "Guys will be like sweet, there's a girl in the men's room."

"Point taken."

The men's room door is literally right next to me, and none of the foyer jabronis seem to be paying much attention. On the sly, I crack open the door to a restroom with olive-colored walls that smells inexplicably of baby powder with two stalls, two sinks, one urinal, and get me in here before my water breaks.

I open the nearest stall and square off with the toilet. Jess struggles in behind me, trying to get the door shut. I squeeze in to make room and *aw man*, my pants touched the porcelain. Indifferently, Jess manages to bolt the door and falls into the position of big spoon. I feel her breasts against my back and her thighs conforming to my rear, all while our hands are stuck in this cumbersome pink bag.

"Why didn't you pick the handicap stall?" Her voice is echoey and a little high-strung.

"Too far away." I unzip my fly…*Nothing doing*. The hose is out but the tap won't run.

"What's going on up there?" Jess pokes her head under my arm. "Stage fright?"

"Yes, thank you." *It's a drought*. "Watching doesn't help."

"How about now?" She presses on my stomach from inside the backpack.

"Eee-yo-okay." *Off to the races*.

This is the second-best feeling in the whole wide—*door!*

The men's room door just opened! I step in front of Collin where my arms go over his head in a complicated dance move in order to climb the toilet. Losing momentum halfway, he hoists me up the rest of the trip. My feet are on the black seat, my butt on the chrome pipe, and my hair against the teal tiles. Yes, this feels like Twister, and all the while Collin is still peeing. I can see his ding-ding, and shift my eyes to something kindlier, like this extraordinary green wall.

The newcomer steps up to the urinal directly outside the partition. His brown suede shoes take a stance, and then *he's* off to the races. We're neck and neck and *oh, dear God.* Brown suede shoes? Gold buckle? It's Professor Walluski! Stricken with fear, I broadcast a warning and let Jess mark my face. She examines me quizzically.

Why does he look so constipated? Ex-Lax. He wants Ex-Lax. No, he wants Tums. I think we overreacted IMHO. I jumped up here and now my jeans are wet. Worried. He's worried. About what?

I guide her sightline down underneath the divider and mouth *Walluski*. Receiving the message, she peels her eyes off his shoes in utter horror.

OhmyGodohmyGodohmyGodohmyGod.

Did he see her Nikes? With those big, loopy shoelaces? Does he recognize my Chucks? Nah, no way. Everyone has these shoes. Then again, he did have two long hours to memorize them.

There's nothing we can do! Nothing we can do but wait him out!

Jess and I breathe heavily down each other's necks, and, of course, my stage fright is back. At least *one* of us can go. Walluski luxuriates, savoring the moment, shifting his feet minutely to shake off the dew. Then, out of nowhere, he takes a full step back while one foot leaves the floor, followed by the sound of a flushing toilet. Did he just high kick the urinal?

There's no time to wonder because he's already in motion. Water rushes from the sink, picking up where the toilet left off. I hear the whirr of the soap dispenser and the rubbing of hands, each disturbance making our eyes dart around in fear as we attempt to decode his movements. The faucet turns. A paper towel buzzes out of the machine. Then a soft crumpling of tissue. Then nothing. He's in here. I know he's still in here. I clear the saliva from my mouth in earnest. Quietly, the door to the foyer swings open, and sways closed, returning the room to silence.

Jess is basically leaning on me. "Is he gone?" she whispers in my ear.

I tip her back. "I think so." A sheen of sweat glistens on her face in the light.

"I knew we should've used the girl's room." She blows a stray hair from her eyes.

I tuck myself in and help my queen off her throne. "I bet you he's posted right outside the door too."

"Collin." Jess huffs. "If he catches us, all that trouble will have been for nothing." She punctuates her statement with a boot to the toilet handle.

"I'm thinking." I meditate to the flow of draining water, then snap my fingers. "I know. I'll text some friends to distract him." I slide out my phone and hit the on-button and…it's not turning on.

"Dead?" asks Jess. "Fantastic."

A third voice reverberates off the walls. "Is there a *girl* in here?"

He must've come in when our toilet flushed. Jess and I freeze, exchanging blank stares at one another like deer in the headlights. Why do deer do that, anyway? Don't they know how to cross the street properly yet? Cars have been around since like the 1890s. Those deer have to move. Move deer! We have to move!

I reach out for the bolt on the door and whisper, "I don't think it's Willaby."

It's Walluski, you imbecile, which I am way too scared to say out loud. So instead I grab Collin's wrist with my able hand and stop him. There we pause, hands levitating, seemingly forever. I close my eyes in thought. *I don't know.* The voice was deep and guttural, but not gruff, if that makes sense. It didn't have that Walluski style, his flair. And the tone. This voice sounded more curious than vengeful. I open my eyes. Our hands are shaking, from one part suspense, two parts alcohol withdrawal. The time has come. I have to shit or get off the pot, so I exhale, and let go.

Collin slides out the lock and reveals us to, *relief-sigh*, only another student. It's some thugged out guy in a North Carolina fitted cap and sleeveless hoodie, probably a junior.

"Oh shit!" His hand flies to his mouth.

"Hey, Tar Heel guy," Collin starts. "Was there a teacher outside that looked like he was waiting for someone?"

"Yeah, Mr. Walluski. He's lookin' at his watch. What's the deal with that guy?"

I step alongside Collin. "He didn't send you in here to spy on us, did he?"

"Oh shit! Y'all are still handcuffed together? That's crazy!" Collin's new friend claps once loudly in awe and glances at the exit. "Na, I don't talk to that dude. I had him in the fall."

I cast a glare at my co-Brockportian—Brockportite?—Brockporter?—*sure*—who seems to know more about me than I do about him. Either that or he can travel through time and see through pink backpacks. I do not like where this is headed, but I must know.

"What do you mean by *still?*"

Tar Heel looks at me dumbfounded. "Y'all haven't seen Facebook yet?"

Oh God no. Cue *Psycho* shower scene music. Close-up on Collin. Close-up on me. Close-up on this asshole. God, those violins are haunting. My life is ruined. This has Duncan's name written all over it, exacting his revenge mercilessly upon me. Here comes the cello part. *Dun-duhhh. Dun-duhhhh.*

"Are you serious?" I corner Tar Heel against the wall. "Someone posted photos of us on Facebook?"

Collin's new friend is getting intimidated. Good. I have him right where I want him.

"Uh, yeah," says Tar Heel, grinning. "Photos."

Collin reels me in, but I jerk free and reclaim my lost footing so that I may better loom over Tar Heel.

"Did I say photos?" asks Tar Heel. "Make that a video!" *Apparently, I misjudged.* He can't contain his enthusiasm a minute longer. "Maaan, Jess, Collin, you cats are famous!" He busts out his phone and points at it with his E.T. finger. "You got six thousand four hundred and eighty-two likes and two angries. Haters."

I don't know what the fuck he just said, but it's got to wait. I have to get Jess back on track before Professor Walluski barges back in here and murders her.

"Oh, and about one hundred thirteen comments." Tar Heel fist pumps his phone and brings it to his nose. "There's this one crazy jockstrap on here trollin' hard. Duncan somebody."

"This is a nightmare," says Jess. "I'm in a nightmare."

"Who's Duncan?" I ask. "He sounds like a jabroni."

"He looks like one too," says Tar Heel, squinting at the screen.

"He's some guy I was seeing," says Jess. "I broke it off a few days ago. He wants to own me. He's insane."

"Now when a man loves a woman—" Tar Heel begins some parable, and *yeah*. "Oh! I love that song!—When a may-yan loves a woemuhhhn—"

I cut him off. "That's nice. Do you think you can do us a favor and distract your old teacher?"

"The moral of the story is possessing someone is bad. Slavery's evil. Make peace, not war. Ya feel me?"

"Yup. So you'll help?"

"For a selfie, I will!" Tar Heel jumps between me and Jess, camera held high. "Get the bling out. Don't be shy now. Show me the bling!"

Jess and I take our hands out of the backpack, pretending to strangle him.

"Uhhh! Holla!" He holds his thumb down for a photo burst. "Jess, smile, baby. You look mortified. You only live once, girl. Yay-yahhh!" He lowers the phone and backs away. "Instant up-load. So, what I gotta do to Walluski? Rob his ass? Just playin'. I'm a good person."

"Just…draw him away from the men's room," I say, "to the exit right outside the door. Then, we can sneak out the other way to the courtyard exit. Strike up a conversation, keep him talking, and make sure he keeps his back to us. And whatever you do, don't look at us when we come out."

"Got it," says Tar Heel.

"But first," says Jess. "Show me the video."

"We don't have time for this," I say.

"I will see this video, even if we have to make a detour to the library."

Tar Heel thumb-taps on his phone. "Heading…for…Drake."

"No, we're not." I lay down the law. "Enough chatter. Tar Heel, you're up."

We follow him to the exit where he stops at the door, does some military-eyeball hand signal, performs a marine-wave toward the trenches, and marches out.

Jess looks down. "Gonna zip that yourself this time, big guy?"

"Yes, ma'am." I zip up. *Okay, game time.* This is almost going to be more difficult than the test.

Walluski's voice is coming in clear: "I don't often eat at McDonald's, no."

This has got to be one clean break. I can't crack the door to check his line of sight. I just have to go for it. It's nearly twenty feet from here to the exit leading into the courtyard. It'll take about thirty seconds to walk down the foyer, past the snack shop, and get through the door. Thirty seconds Tar Heel has to maintain a conversation. Thirty seconds that Walluski won't whip his head around. Yeah, we're not gonna make it, but to hell with it.

Collin grabs my hand inside the backpack and opens the door to the foyer where Tar Heel is spinning a tale.

"So there I was waiting in line, and I'm like dang, where my McGangbang at? So they gave me a toy to play with while I waited. All's I ordered was. What'd I order? Oh yeah, a chicken sandwich with lettuce. That's let-tuce. Iceberg. No mayo. That's no mayo-nnaise on the burger just the balls cuz I keep it gangster, feel me? Combinized with a double cheese-burger, which is two meat pat-ays and a slice of Grade A American ched-dar. What I cleanse the palate with? Don't tell me now. Don't tell me. Milkshake! That's milk-shake chocolate, in my bedroom, not in the yard. You know they put plastic in those, right?"

I can see Walluski's combover out of my peripheral and the courtyard exit straight ahead. I let the men's room door close without a sound, save for my heart thundering in my ears. Collin starts to tiptoe along the wall, but that's no good. If Tar Heel's eyes wander to us for a millisecond, that'll tip off Walluski and we're toast. Forget his eyes, his conversation's about as exciting as an infant taking a shit. It won't hold for long, so I smack Collin on the butt to move it.

"Son, I really don't have time for your drive-thru experience."

He's gonna turn.

"Drive-thru? Man, I work there."

We're almost to the corner. Don't stop. Collin, why are you stopping? Because the diversion stopped, *oh no*. For real, Tar Heel? It's finished. Any second Walluski'll catch us. Our careers are—

"Now I remember you. From last semester. You did very well in my class. Aced the final, if I recall. You know what? Let me buy you a fruit cup. Harrison Hall makes a memorable fruit cup."

I tap Collin on the butt again, and we take off all stealthy and B2 bomber-like. However, silent as we are, my heart still goes haywire, a rising and falling scale of BPMs, which doesn't taper off until I pass into the café area. From there, we jog out through the courtyard doors where I can finally get some oxygen to my brain.

Bullet—

—dodged.

Thanks for the assist, fellow lavatory patron. Now where to? Ah yes, to the art building. Jess leads me by a length, seeming to have forgotten our destination, because she's leading us straight toward Brown, which just so happens to connect with Drake Library.

"Um, the art building is this way, dear." I point north.

"We are taking a detour." Jess brims her eyes with her hand. "To Drake."

"That's no detour," I say. "You want to check Facebook."

"Don't you?" asks Jess.

"Yeah, but, prioritize." I hold out my hands like two pans of a scale. "Social life." I shake my hand in the backpack at Brown. "Or handcuffs off." I shake my free hand at the far away art room. "Basic much?"

Jess stops and takes one tough look at me. She starts to say words and things, but I lose track of the meaning. My mind is busied by the super-basic at 12 o'clock coming in hot, her midriff a golden brown spool, unthreaded to clothe the rest of her with an open top and denim shorts, below which strut her caramelized legs, as her black hair ripples in her wake from above, a mirage of a gypsy stepped out of an Arabian night. Destiny has sent her to me.

And placed her at my side in a sun chair to rub my chest. Her beach nymphs gather around, wearing bikinis made of hundred-dollar bills, to fan us with palm branches. The overturning of the ocean fills my ears and the RumChata fills my mouth. Life is paradise, shattered when a figure blocks my light. It's my butler, in full tux, bearing an antique telephone on a silver tray.

"What is it, Rupert?"

"Your wife is calling, sir."

I lower my Jack Nicholson Ray-Bans to make sure I heard correctly. "I have a wife?"

"Jess Marshall."

"Oh yes, the wife." I withdraw the gypsy's arm from my body and dig my toes into the sand, slightly riled.

"She wants to know how your business trip is going. Shall I tell her you're having a dalliance?"

"Hmmm." I set down the hollowed coconut with my bendy straw inside, steeple my fingers to my chin, then look up. "What's a dalliance?"

"A polite word for ruthlessly banging innumerable coke whores, sir."

"Rupert." I shoot him my index finger. "Do not say dalliance."

"Very good, sir, but I must tell her something."

Rupert is right. I've got to say something. I must use my charm and secure this girl's number. She walks so fast. Quick, make a move.

"Hi." I hail her. "My sister and I were discussing her life goals, and I'm looking for an outside opinion."

Oh my God, what is he doing? This chick stopped dead in her tracks to hear this?

"—so, what do you think?" asks Collin. "Art room to remove handcuffs or library to see video?"

"Tough call." The girl holds her chin and Turkish accent. "You have me curious about the video. Though tempting as it is, I've got to say art room. The video can always wait."

Collin nudges me in the side. "See. Told you."

"That's not fair. You didn't present it right." I check my invisible watch. "Are we done here?"

"Almost," says Collin. "I have an idea." He turns back to the swimsuit model, way out of his league. "Why don't I take down your number, and we can both watch the video later over coffee?"

"Yeah," she says, "that sounds great."

!!!!

Where did these balls come from? And she's actually giving him the light of day! Why do I care? Why am I caring? He's handcuffed to me. *You can't have him!*

"My phone is dead at the moment," says Collin. "However, I do have my lucky pencil handy." He unzips the backpack and takes out my lucky Rainbow Dash pencil. "Ooph. No paper though. You got any?"

The model, known from this day forward as *That Hoe Over There*, pats her pockets in search of stationary. "Zilch."

Collin turns to me. "Jess, be a doll and remember these digits."

What!? Like hell I'm remembering these stinking digits.

"We're ready," says Collin.

The thot recites her number: "585-553-2425."

Collin turns to me. "Got that, Jess?"

"Got it."

"Okay, now repeat it back."

"1-800-Lick-My-Labes."

"I think you're missing some 5s." Collin turns to his thot in question. "You know what? I'll find you online. Your name is?"

"Marissa Aldemir."

"Collin Marshall." He shakes her hand and I pull him away.

"Good luck with the handcuffs," she says. "Thanks," he says. "It's been real."

Real lame.

Real cool, Jess. Thanks for the cock block. And why are we still heading toward Drake? You heard Esmeralda. She said no.

"You worry too much about reputation." I duck under a Frisbee. "About what people think."

"Me?" Jess glances back. "How about you? You've been status-seeking all day for that analyst job."

"The job's not for me," I say. "It's for my parents."

"Living the life they want you to?"

"What? No. I love finance. I mean the money I would earn is for them."

"Huh." Jess knits her brow. "Why is that?"

"They slaved for me to come to this school." We take shelter from the heat beneath the shade of the trees. "I figure I pay them back."

"Why not use financial aid?"

"Too much interest." I rub my fingers. "They'd be left in even more debt."

"Wow," she says, amazedly. "I never thought your ego was capable of caring like that for somebody else."

"I helped you, didn't I?"

"Yes, and I thanked you for it. This thing with your parents though. It only helps them. It's much more noble I think."

"That makes two of us. According to my mother," *and I don't know why I'm saying this, but,* "I'm on the lam from CPS and need to pay the family rent so they don't come to collect me again. Crazy, right?"

"Yeah, crazy," Jess says, unassured. "They'd be a little late, wouldn't they?"

"In theory."

"How did you become fugitive the first time?"

"My dad was broke and my mom was drunk."

She drops the flippant tone. "How old were you?"

"Five."

"That must've been difficult," she says, sympathetically.

"Can't win 'em all." *Subject change.* "What about you?" I ask. "Why teach kindergarten? Dad run out of money?"

"No." Jess scoffs. "My grandmother, who passed away for

real, taught kindergarten for 34 years, and I always admired her for it. Also, I love kids."

"Yeah?"

"Yeah. It's so much fun. Like parading them around in their costumes for Halloween. Stamping the floor with reindeer hooves to pretend like Rudolph was there, and—I know making shoebox dioramas and school buses out of egg cartons might not mean much to you, but it makes a heap of difference to me. Grandma Fisher's kids would come back to her years later and say how much she had affected them. Kids from broken homes. Kids from good homes. Even the ones who wet their pants and watch *Spice World*." Jess winks at me.

"My favorite pastimes."

We've been talking for so long, we're already at the entrance to Brown, staring at our own reflections, in which I can see myself blushing.

"I don't care about the video only for my benefit," says Jess. "It's for theirs too."

"Fine." I relent. "But I cannot be held responsible for anything that occurs on this alleged detour."

"Okay." Jess smiles, happily. "I'm good with that."

I should have jangled my cuffed hand at the art building for emphasis and shook my empty hand at Brown to represent nothing. That would've sold her.

I am woman, on a mission. Nothing will stand in my way. We cut through Brown to a glass enclosure which leads out to the pedestrian bridge, and why is that model chick thot still on my mind? How did Collin hitting on her possibly sting me like it did? I trek up the bridge's slope, searching my feelings, and glance out the bank of windows overlooking the parking lot, as if the bright rows of cars will give me the answer. Am I jealous? *Moi? Jealous?* Over what? The egotistical Collin Marshall? **Self-aware-sigh** I suppose I could back up and look at the man objectively. He did say he wants to provide for his parents, so he must have a heart in there somewhere. *Gah.* Maybe there's hope for this Tin Man after all. But, for the record, I possess zero jealousy. Why have we stopped?

Alicia is pacing at the bottom of the bridge, talking on her cell phone. We're at the peak of the walkway directly above the railroad. I couldn't see the Drake side before because of the grade of the bridge, or I would never have let us get this far. Alicia doesn't pace now. She lingers, though hasn't spotted me. Yet.

"You know that ex-girlfriend I used to have?" I ask.

"You mean from *this morning*?" Jess replies.

"Yes, her. She's right there. Redhead, white shirt. Let's take a shortcut."

I carousel us around and walk back the way we came.

"What does she want?" Jess asks.

"Who knows? Who cares." We only steal a few paces when Jess grabs my wrist with the fear of death.

"Stop."

I look around, confused and worried. "Why?"

Why is right. Why here? Why now? And me with no door to hide behind.

"What is it?" Collin persists.

I nod to the Brown side. "See that guy in the red shirt and jean shorts? Buzz-cut, 6'3". That's Duncan. If he sees you with me, he's going to start swinging."

"You're joking, right?"

I glance out the window, getting the sudden urge to take my chances with the three-story drop.

"Jess?"

I shake my head nervously. "I wish."

"But we're at school," says Collin. "I'm sure the threat of expulsion will stop him from hitting me."

"Collin, he's a nut job," I say. "His anger issues have anger issues."

I'm glad Jess loved herself enough to kick this Duncan guy to the curb. Not so glad he didn't stay there.

"Right," I say, confidently. "It's time to man up then." I steer us back toward Alicia waiting on the Drake side.

I don't blame you, Collin. Let's get the hell out of here. You can be the Tin Man and the Cowardly Lion all you want. The Lion doesn't need courage anyway because he's not a real lion. The Lion is just a man in makeup. Collin, really, you can play all the parts, and Dorothy too, because you just wanted to go home, and I should've listened to you.

We're a dozen feet from the end of the bridge when Alicia looks up from her phone and approaches.

"There you are, you drunken piece of shit." She stops right in front of us.

Bystanding jabronis and basic girls slow their rolls to watch.

"Oh! Alicia. Hi!" I wave hello, motioning to Jess. "This is my cousin, Shawna."

"You make out with your cousin!?" Alicia folds her arms. "She's from Europe."

"I've seen the video!" says Alicia.

"That video is highly interpretive."

Alicia rips the pink backpack out from between us. "Is it?" The cuffs glimmer in the light.

"Look," I say. "Official or unofficial. It's over. It was my fault. And, hey, it was only two weeks. We didn't waste that much time."

"That's how you see it?" Her tone is full of scorn. "As a waste of time?"

"I was thinking more of you with that comment."

She pushes mae. "Dick. Two weeks to me is a long time."

So is four years. "For what it's worth, I'm sorry. I got the memo from Carl. There's nothing more to argue."

"There's plenty," says Alicia. "You humiliated me in public with this…this whore!"

I open hand slap Alicia in the side of her head on impulse. She lets the backpack fall and goes for my hair. The pulling hurts like hell, but I tolerate the pain long enough to grab her ponytail with my free hand and slug her in the gut with my left, Collin coming right along with me.

A forming circle of jabronis begins to cheer. Jess is literally taking her shot at the title. I mean, come on! She's fighting my ex!

No one talks to me like that.

Right then, someone taps me on the shoulder. I turn as a fist grazes my chin. *Duncan!* I jab him in the face out of self-preservation, square on the nose. He staggers back checking for blood, which he finds, and now he's furious.

Alicia clings to my hair, ripping at the roots. I spin a quarter turn to shake this daffy bitch off me, and throw in a few swipes for good measure.

I try to ignore getting scratched at and stepped on and maintain focus. Duncan comes at me once more. He feints left; I wind back a right hook but can't deliver. Jess yanks my fist back farther than I plan so she can crack on Alicia, leaving me wide open! I see it coming and can do nothing but wince as Duncan socks me in the eye.

flash

Oh no. Collin just went down, smack against the concrete. His arm is limp, my left hand useless. I'm forced to fight Alicia with my right, snaking it around her neck to lock her in a choke hold. Out of the tail of my eye, I see Duncan crouch next to Collin raring to give him another shot. He wants to mess him up bad. I swing Alicia about and kick Duncan away. It's not enough, but thankfully a good Samaritan, and a chunky one at that, shoves him even harder, and this time Duncan falls.

Two Duncans rise up off the ground and charge me. I prepare for them to strike, but then two basic girls with Frappuccinos yell—"Security's coming!"—and the Duncans bolt.

University Police? That's the last thing we need. I let go of Alicia's neck and let her crawl to her feet.

"Ow." I roll onto my back. Every nerve in my cheekbone feels crunched. "Where's security?"

"Down there." The basic girl points out a window. "A guard is watching from the parking lot."

Alicia picks up the backpack. "I'm taking this as a souvenir, so it can remind me of how much of an asshole you were!" She hobbles away, up the bridge.

Jess helps me up to paparazzi galore. Ladies and jabronis gather around with their smart-phones aimed directly at us like we're celebrities at a press conference.

"Damn." Jess rests her hand on her hip and nods to Alicia. "Someone needs a new tamp string."

Our fan club laughs their asses off and starts handing out back-pats. Jess appears to be soaking in the limelight, less mortified than before. At the peak of the bridge, Alicia about faces and shoots Jess a look that can fire laser beams. Is she coming back for seconds? Nope, but Jess blows her a goodbye kiss.

Keep walking, Sally.

Well, she's ghost. In other news, the guy who rescued me from Duncan examines my eye and gives me a nudge. "Bad luck, Helen."

"Thanks ref," I tell him. *Hey, it's the guy from the exam.* He had the chubby voice, and now I can see that he has a chubby body to go with it; Chubroni.

"You've got a shiner." Jess covers her mouth. "I am so, so sorry."

"Uhh." I stumble forward, probing my cheek. "I love how they took it out on the wrong people. You would think they'd be mad at us."

"I know!" says Jess. "So immature."

"For real."

"Don't worry," says Jess. "We'll get some ice for you as soon as we can."

"After we see the Facebook video."

"Collin, I'm surprised.""We paid the toll. Might as well."

The crowd disperses, seeming to collectively remember the security guard. Jess and I follow suit, and hurry into the open alcove surrounding Drake while Chubroni keeps us company.

Olgh. I clutch my stomach. Alicia must've slugged me harder than I thought. Walk it off, Jess. Walk it off. My life is at stake here. Game face.

"Savage party I threw last night, huh?" asks Chunk.

This guy is from the Athenian Forest.

"You're telling me." Collin pokes at his bruise.

I cover my bases. "You think Walluski saw the video?"

"Not a chaaance," says Chunk.

Is he looking down Jess's top or is that just me?

This guy is totally staring at my tits.

"And if Walluski did see it," he continues, "who's going to flunk the Handcuff Couple?"

"The what?" I peel down my lower lip and boost up my top.

"The Handcuff Couple. Bonnie and Clyde. That's your

nicknames." Chunk tilts up his chin like the time just expired on his coin-operated binoculars. "Kids will be talking about this for years." He breaks from our path. "I'll see ya 'round this weekend. 201 Erie Street, be there, be circle. And bring the cuffs again. They're a riot."

"We can't get them off," I say.

"Even better!" He tosses a wave.

Collin and I glance at each other as Chunk bumbles around the stone corridor alongside Drake, heading toward the gym. *Exercise. Good for him.*

We journey through the library's foyer, a prism of flyers, and enter into the main wing, where everything is massive and gray; just a gray blob, truth be told. The most color here is from the banners of the stained-glass décor hanging over the main stairway. To the right, rows of computers are set up in a zigzag partition where students are hard at work on term papers. Jess takes the lead, desperately searching for an empty chair. Taken, taken, taken, IT Help Desk, taken, taken, out of order, taken, hottie, taken, *holy hell*, taken, taken, taken, free!

I lunge for the chair. Half of Collin's ass claims it first, so I give his knee a squeeze, and, ticklish, he leaps to the carpet, where he stays put, crouched low, while I type in my username, *jfisher1*, followed by a password, *CampusQueen19*, which I guard with my life. Up pops Internet Explorer and Facebook and a picture of me and Collin in a men's room with a guy named Javon Hewitt, alias Tar Heel. And how cute? He captioned the photo too: *If you want they autograph theyre heading for Drake #nottherapper #notthemaleduckneither #bitches.*

"That explains how our exes found us."

"Looks that way," says Jess. "I've gotta admit though, Collin. I'm surprised you actually turned a woman down."

"And I never knew you to tell a guy like that off."

"You think I'm some kind of doormat?" she asks.

"Yeah, and that's clearly what you think of me."

Jess slowly removes her hand from the mouse.

"I was a doormat," she confides, "once upon a time. But I'm not *now*."

"It's so different from what I hear around school. From what I realized I saw in Music Listening."

"That's the outdated Wikipedia version." She takes a breath. "I was tired of being used."

"Same." I look her in the eye and go out on a limb. "Maybe we dropped the false perceptions we had for each other last night."

She looks at the computer. "I think we dropped all perception."

The illicit video graces the screen in all its infamy. *Handcuff Couple* heads the top of the box. The first frame is black. We're both tagged in it, and Javon Tar Heel wasn't exaggerating. There are over a thousand likes and hundreds of shares. This thing has gone viral.

We're working with some basic girl numbers here, far too much stimulation for my brain to absorb. I mean, just above that is a post from her Schipperke. Yes, her dog has got his own account, and he just posted a status update about a new leash.

Who's the original uploader on this vid? Carl Iversen. Why is that name familiar?

Goddamnit, Carl! What happened last night? Let me just access my subconscious here for a minute…oh okay, I dragged him into the party with me. He tried to leave before the two hours were up, which we *agreed* upon. I stopped him. And that's all I'm able to recall as Jess's finger hovers anxiously over the mouse.

Judgement Day.

I'm scared to watch this.

A crowd dances under multicolored lights in a living

room lined with couches. Sitting on the nearest couch is my pink backpack, surrounded by Relax Riesling.

Of a basic vintage. Only the best, naturally.

"I can't hear anything." So I turn up the volume.

While she fiddles with that, I glance away for a moment, above the partition, long enough to catch two University Police officers strutting into the library. *Christ.* I go from a crouch to a dive, straight into the cubby beneath the desk.

Why is he under there? Did I miss something?

"Police," I whisper.

"WHO'S YOUR DADDY!? WHO'S YOUR DADDY!?" Jess-from-last-night belts her new catchphrase out of the speakers while Jess-from-right-now bungles with the volume knob, all of which gives me a start.

Oh, dear God. She's slapping the keyboard.

ALT-F4's not working!

Yes, finally, grab the mouse and pause the video.

I whisper, "Close one," below deck and pat Collin on the head.

She may as well have played the *Cops* theme song at full throttle because from inside my hidey-hole, I can see them coming this way. At least, I think they are. I can just make out the shadows of their boots through the narrow slit at the bottom of the desk. Yup, they're combing the area. And they carry guns and arrest people just like the real police.

To be honest, I'd have preferred two mall cops. All this running from law enforcement and impersonating the disabled is going to give me a heart attack. If we want to keep our futures on lock, we have to get off campus ASAP. *Oh God.* They're in our row, walking their rounds from station to station like they're checking cells on a prison block.

Play it cool, Jess. Cool as a kumquat, a kumquat who just minimized the Facebook window and is now typing casually on Word right-handed.

I coil up like an armadillo, bundled in front of Jess, hidden behind her legs. Her left hand settles covertly under the table to give the illusion she's relaxed like Riesling, just as an officer strolls up to her.

The pressure of being watched is all too real. For a split second I think he's going to drag Collin out by his pantlegs. I don't even look, and I don't dare speak. If the school finds out I was in a fight, they will reject the shit out of my application for graduating. I am immersed in my typing. Type and breathe. That is all I do. Boring. It's all so boring. Who wants to be here? No one. Not even the officer, who mumbles "Fucking millennials" and, repelled by unholy boredom, moves onto the next student.

Two minutes pass. My butt is sore. Nothing else to report.

"Coast is clear."

I crawl out of the cubby, wondering what police would even do to us. In Jess's defense, Alicia did call her a whore and steal her property. And me? Self-defense. Dunkaccino swung first. Still, I rather not risk it. I want to hear the "Pomp and Circumstance" echo from the rafters. I can almost hear it now, and I think I do. But nope, that's the video. Jess hit resume.

Chunk is on the outside of the crowd in a Viking helmet

going nuts. The dancers fan out, creating a perimeter, where Collin and I take center stage handcuffed, grinding and twerking.

This is the video? It hardly warrants the thousands of likes we received from the tri-state area. *Never mind.*

I rip open my shirt waving a bottle of Bacardi 151 around like I'm twirling a lasso in a western, with Collin as the horse.

Yee-haw?

I bite my nails to the quick.

Internet-Jess unclips her bra and out pop the sweater cows. *Now it's a party!*

This is a dream. I am dreaming. I have slumbered here while these visions did appear. Those are someone else's boobs.

"It's not so bad," I say, like a director in the editing room. "You barely notice them."

Jess deadpans. "Is that supposed to be a compliment?"

"I'm sure everyone noticed them. You look great."

"Keep digging." Jess turns back and refastens her eyes to the screen, right when her online cohort proceeds to dry hump me from behind, shouting an emphatic, "Who's your mother's husband, bitch!?"

Her voice flies through the speakers unexpectedly loud, inviting neighboring students to poke their heads up from their stations and see what's going on. At that moment, the head librarian, withered and frail, practically a zombie, halts her gait in our row to join in the viewing.

"Don't take that, Drunk Collin! Do something!"

As if my past self can hear my plea, I whirl around and pin Drunk Jess onto her back, our limbs mangled in a knot. I press my lips to hers and repay her in equally rhythmic dry humps. People in the crowd die from uncontrollable fits of laughter, the video eliciting a lesser response from the eavesdroppers in the library.

Untag. Untag. Untag. Untag!

She clicks in such a frenzy that nothing happens, and the cursor lands over the angry face emoji. *What the—*. Two people rated it angry: Duncan, go figure, and it just had to be, none other than, Bruce Fisher, Jess's father.

My sinking heart cements me to the floor as the video fades to black. Somewhere in the aisle, the librarian unruffles her dress, coughs at our disruption, most likely from her organs flaking apart internally, and walks on. With the show over, the giraffe-necked students return to their work, leaving me alone to kneel, somberly, fully realizing why my boss, Mike, had let me go. Because Bruce Fisher told him to. Late or not, I would've lost my job regardless.

This is the scandal I've dreaded. Now I get why Duncan was so pissed. *Well, not really, but still.* The video rendered his naughty picture of me completely moot. *OMFG*—What will my Brockport friends think? And my friends from yoga? And the girls at the salon? And my friends from South Beach? And Martha's Vineyard? And my New York people? What if MLK Elementary gets ahold of this? Or my back-up schools? Or the dean? What's Collin so bent out of shape for? His popularity just went stratospheric. He doesn't care what people think of him anyway. Even if he did, the accounting department is full of sleazeballs. He has nothing to lose.

"Your dad won't rehire me." I tap the angry icon. "He's the one who got me fired."

Jess opens her mouth, caught off guard, and locks her eyes with mine.

"It's okay," she consoles me, touching my hand. "I know my dad. This was only his wasabi reaction. That's what Mom calls it. He freaks the same way whenever Snowcone poos on the rug. Once he cools down, you'll see—"

"Jess." My face is numb. "I don't think I will *see*. Fired is fired."

"Collin," she mimics. "You helped me get through my

exam and took a punch to the face you didn't deserve. I'll explain everything to him. I owe you that, no matter what. I won't hold you hostage from here on out."

"You're too kind." I hold up a finger to prevent her from interjecting, but then sigh audibly and give in. "All right. It's worth a shot."

"And your face will heal up, good as new," she adds.

"You're right," I say, my spirits brightening. "Sure, things are bad, but it's no reason to ruin a perfectly good day."

"I wouldn't say all that." I glance at the uploader's name again. "Your little pal, Carl, is a dead man."

"Not if I kill him first. Bastard cost me my job."

I go to delete *Handcuff Couple* from my wall, not knowing how I'm ever going to recuperate.

"Wait," says Collin. "I saw something weird near the end. You know, aside from the impromptu striptease." He covers my hand and repositions the cursor. "Hit replay."

"Itching for another look?" I raise an eyebrow, vaguely aghast.

"Please."

"Okay, keep your pants on." I left-click. "Ya pervy scoundrel."

"Fast forward…stop there."

I freeze the frame, of me riding Collin topless. Unamused, I roll my chin in a circle until my gaze lands on his big dumb mug. "Really?"

"There." He points to a girl in the background slipping her hand into my backpack on the couch. "Who is that?"

"Is that Britney?" I blow up the video to full screen. "It is, that traitor."

She has one hand pressed to her bangs in embarrassment and the other trapped in a three-inch zipper compartment below the pouch.

"Rewind a few seconds." Collin slides his finger across the monitor.

I run it back, hit play, and watch events unfold. Britney fishes into her pocket, then takes out her hand, thumb against forefinger, and deposits something into my bag.

I drop my jaw and turn to Jess, her face a mirror image. "The key!" we exclaim in unison.

"That girl is so dead," she declares.

"It was in there the whole time!?" I rub my mouth and look to Jess, who is growing a Grinchy smile from ear to ear. "No. No. We are not going after that thing. No way in hell."

"Then what?" Jess asks. "The art room?"

"The gym is closer." I nod to my side. "We can borrow a pair of lock cutters."

"From who?" she asks. "I don't want to have to explain things. More and more people are recognizing us as the day goes on."

I hold up a finger, letting my eyes drift from side to side. "I got it." I open a new browser, log into my email and enter my password—

J***L*W.

Jess twists her mouth in a grin. "Wow."

"What?" I ask.

"I think you have a man crush," she observes. "A big fat one."

"I do not. He's a respectable, two-time Academy Award-nominated actor."

"And you want to kiss him," she says. "On the mouth."

"What!?" I smother her crooked smile. "Okay, that's enough out of you, Kesha." She licks my palm. "Ah!" I pull it away fast. "Slobber."

She puckers her lips and makes a kissing sound.

Great. "I'm messaging Carl to bring us a metal file."

"Is he going to bake it in a cake?" Jess asks, mischievously. "Low-fat, red velvet please."

"Shhh. Let's hope he responds." I hear a *bing*. "Yes! He wrote back."

> *Carl Iverson: You haven't gotten them off yet? Rendezvous at Smith Hall, room 208, second floor. I'm making up a lab, and I've got the perfect tool.*
>
> *P.S. Your ex-girlfriend is on campus looking for you.*

"So helpful, he is," I say, tongue firmly in cheek.

"Collin. Smith Hall is by Edwards. UP is looking for us. How are we supposed to get there?"

"Improvise," he says. "There's a parking lot downstairs. Lot W. We make it there, I'm sure we can bum a ride."

I can already tell this is another one of his wacky schemes, but he does get results.

"Fine." I skip over to Facebook. "I'm telling Britney to meet us in Smith after her thistory final gets out."

"The what final?" he asks.

"It's a tongue-twister."

"No, it's not."

I extend my middle finger and continue typing.

I don't think Jess likes the idea of playing it off the cuff—*such a shitty pun*—but what choice do we have? She ends her session and rises from the chair.

Ow, okay. My stomach pain is back. No need for alarm. *Walk it off. Walk it off.*

I pick myself up off the floor when a basic girl openly gawks from one section down. To counter, I take Jess's hand in mine. The girl looks away.

"Feeling affectionate?" Jess asks, with a prick in her voice.

"We need a diversion so people don't stare at the cuffs."

"I don't know." She forces a laugh. "I think your raccoon eye is fairly diverting."

"I guess we have two diversions then." I walk her down the aisle.

"Why don't I just stick my hand down your pants and go for a third?"

"That, is the most sensible thing you've said all day." My smirk fades.

Something is seriously wrong.

It feels like somebody put cold hands on my stomach and is wringing it into a wet noodle the more I move.

Jess's face turns green. With haste, I loop us out of the aisle and around the back of the big staircase. My arm around her neck for support, we make it to the first floor, where down the hall, we see the light at the end of the tunnel.

"Hold it in, babe. We're almost outside."

The light is a blur. I feel it coming. *Gotta hold on. Gotta hold on.* Why am I about to puke? Nerves? Stress? The unspecified amount of liquor I drank last night? *Oh Gawd.* I hope I'm not pregnant. Did a swimmer get through?

We burst through the door to the outside world, where I lead Jess onto the sidewalk at the corner of the building. Upchuck imminent, I hold back her hair and she boots all over the grass. The smell. The taste. It's in the air. *Ick*, like an acidic peanut buttery orange soda. My stomach is weak.

I wipe my mouth on the back of my hand. Dad is strict Roman Catholic. He doesn't believe in babies out of wedlock. I already foresee what he'll do.

Flouting tradition, I stand at the altar alone, shackled to the floor, in my white Dior dress and seven-foot train, already derailed, staring out at the Fishers and Serventinos on the left, and the Marshalls and God knows what other bottom feeders on the right. Yes, even the seating chart has been flipped. The guests are aware, probably, if the offhand remarks and tilting of heads are any proof.

The doors at the back of the cathedral open, and all rise. Typically, the father of the bride is supposed to walk his daughter down the aisle, but Dad is indisposed, another tradition broken. "Here Comes the Bride" plays as scheduled. In walks Collin, bound and gagged, with the muzzle of a .22-gauge shotgun rammed up against his spine, carried by the architect of this whole bullshit wedding himself, Daddy dearest.

Collin looks washed out, like he's been sleeping in a van with a bag over his head for the last nine days. Even now, he squints at the light from the stained-glass windows, wearing a dazed look on his face that suggests a futile desire for freedom. It's as if he were a leading man who stepped onto the wrong movie set and whose constant ineptitude has kept him from the A-list. Looking for allies, I glance at my mom to pull the fire alarm or something, but she only shrugs as if to say, *You know your father, darling*. Desperate, I turn to recruit the priest and—Friar Walluski?

He pats his hands over the Bible and nods cordially.

"Friar Walluski, it's me, Miss Fisher."

"Not for long."

"Aren't you going to stop him?" I beg.

"The lover or the madman?"

"The madman!"

"Which one is he? Both have such shaping fantasies."

"The man brandishing the loaded shotgun! Isn't any of this at all strange to you?"

"More strange than true."

"Useless," I mutter.

Collin latches onto the last pew in the aisle, urging his parents to do something. What do Mr. and Mrs. Marshall look like? A fat Collin for his dad and Collin in a wig for his mom, proud parents about to join the upper crust, who have already mortgaged a nice piece of lakeshore property and deny Collin any hope of escape.

Dad pries loose his fingers and cajoles him up the steps before the altar. The men stand one behind the other, Dad's rugged face juxtaposing Collin's pretty boy swagger.

"Dearly beloved," begins Walluski, "we are gathered here today to witness the union of Collin Herbert Marshall and Jessica Karen Fisher in holy matrimony, which is an honorable estate, that is not to be entered into unadvisedly or lightly, but reverently and soberly."

I roll my eyes so hard.

"Do you, Collin, take Jess to be your lawfully wedded wife, to have and to hold, from this day forward, for better, for worse, for richer, for poorer, most likely richer, in sickness and in health, until death do you part?"

Collin adamantly shakes his head no.

Dad pumps the shotgun.

Collin adamantly shakes his head yes.

"I do," says Dad, speaking for him, in his deep baritone.

Walluski rejoices ecstatically. "By the power vested in me by the City-State of Athens, I now pronounce you man and wife. You may kiss the bride."

Dad places the gun barrel on Collin's arm and taps him out of the way. Then, moistening his lips, Dad steps forward.

"No no no!" I cry. "I don't want you! You're not Collin! Help! Somebody! Anybody!"

"I object!" Duncan comes running down the aisle. "She's mine!"

I pull away from the attempted kiss, grab the gun, and, just as Duncan steps between us, I fire, issuing a blast, straight through him, into Daddy.

Two bodies drop, and Collin, queasy from the bloodshed—

—vomits into the grass at my side. I rub his back to comfort him while getting a grip myself. I'm spazzing over nothing. Pregnancy symptoms don't come this early. But just in case.

"Collin. Are you Roman Catholic by any chance?"

He spits out the last remnants of puke and stands up,

looking totally perplexed. Totes perplexed. *Oh, it's a perfectly acceptable word. God, don't judge me.*

ACT IV

"My mom used to read the Bible to me as a kid, though I can't say I'm a fan of organized religion. How…how is this relevant?"

"No reason," she says. "Just checking."

On the subject of checking things, I stare at the Venn diagram of blue and orange puke on the lawn, wondering what in the hell my blood sugar level is.

"Are you considering a date here?"

"Um." She ponders the sky.

Date with Collin. Date with Collin. Seriously, what is my sugar level? Okay, I'll go to Smith, lose the cuffs, and go straight home with Britney to grab my kit.

"Well, play your cards right."

"Are we playing Go Fish?" she asks.

"Strip poker."

"Knew you'd say that." She smiles.

I lead her around the corner of Drake and survey the parking lot from the curb. No cars come or go, which puts a hitch in my hiking plan.

"We'll have to wait for a ride," I say.

"Obvi," says Jess.

I look down at her. Would it even work between us? Yeah, she got rid of Duncan, but a tiger doesn't change her stripes that much. She'd get bored.

He can't handle commitment.

She's used to guys who treat her like dog shit. It's too ingrained.

He wants these girls who fall all over him now.

She wants her father.

He's a mama's boy. I can tell. Plus, he might turn back into a puddle of goop.

But she's feisty and sweet and gets my jokes, even when she hated me.

Although, the way he takes charge of situations… Where I see a roadblock, he sees a green light.

But she's a trust fund baby.

He is below the poverty line.

She'll never understand where I come from.

He'll only want me for my money.

And how can I bring home enough bacon to match that nest egg?

You can't go from Ramen to linguine. His head will explode.

It'll never work.

But everything he did today was for his parents.

She does want to help a bunch of kids she hasn't met.

And I admire that. He defends his own.

She might be family-oriented—dating material.

I don't know. Should I try to impress him?

It's a long shot. But, she was the one who turned me down, so I'll just keep doing me.

This is going to be an uphill battle. I have some ground to make up for. To see if he cares.

Assuming the Uni-Po don't nab us first.

"Police are up on the bridge." I point over the parking lot. "They're looking for us."

"Come on." I take her hand and strafe along the side of Drake, hoping to God they don't look down.

We scurry under the bridge and hop into a loading dock. There we camp, concealed from the UP roving overhead. I lean onto the door of a truck protruding from the garage and try to catch my breath. Then, something shiny catches my eye. Some- one left the keys inside.

The underbelly of the bridge stretches out before us, over Lot W—over a pair of dumpsters—over a chain-link fence—trees, tracks, another fence—Lot Q, street, sidewalk, the grass—and smack into Brown.

"If we climb those fences, we can use the bridge for cover. The cops will never see us."

"Or, we borrow this book truck and drive there. The keys are in the ignition."

"I don't feel like adding auto theft to our rap sheet today," says Collin.

"We're not stealing." I clench my hands. "We're borrowing." They pop open. "From the library!"

"A book truck and a book are not the same thing."

He has gotten us this far, and I do want to show him that I'm a team player. "Fine, we'll scale the fences. I hope you appreciate this."

"I do," says Collin, tugging me along. "Good job not breaking the law."

I don't think his ego allows him to thank me very often.

We amble up the ramp, across the parking lot, and skirt around the dumpster—oly shit! Jess and I jump as a shabby old man leaps out with a bag full of bottles and cans. The guy's about to ask for money. Gotta beat him to the punch.

"Hey man, you got a dollar?" I hold out my hand, bracelet hand, to imply felony.

He pulls out his pockets, pats his Fruitopia t-shirt, and, to be thorough, even checks under his train engine hat, stinking to high hell. Jess plugs her nose. *Come on, it can't all be him.* There's rancid milk dripping from the dumpster and moldy pizza crust scattering the ground and, uh, maybe it is him. *Foul.*

"Sorry kids." He comes up empty-handed. "Spent my last green bill on a pinky nail's worth of crack," he squawks, with a toothless grin.

"You see that, Jess?" I gesture to our new friend. "Honesty, with a capital H."

"For halitosis." I step behind Collin and nudge him forward. "You talk to him. He's your people."

"Anything for you, my one percent princess." Collin goes to address Train Hobo Zeke—*I know, he looks like a Zeke*—but then I get inquisitive and cut Collin off.

"Ask Zeke what the engineer hat's for."

"Shhh," Collin says over his shoulder. "He's conducting the dumpster." Collin pauses. "We're calling him Zeke?"

I nod.

"It fits." Collin nods.

It's unclear if Zeke is registering any of this. He just stares at me with an occasional twitch, because that's ordinary social interaction.

"Hello, good sir." I wave at him like a doctor would a coma patient. "You wouldn't by chance know the easiest way through this fence, now would you?" I point to the fence in question, right beside us, to lend him a visual reference.

Zeke hiccups. "Only way through is over the tippy top." He smacks his lips as if rousing from a nap. "And it'll do you good to mind your bees pollen, you doggone butt biscuit."

Jess snorts with laughter.

"You know, Zeke, Jess *is* available." I just go ahead and throw that on out there. "You should ask her for her number."

"You did not just say that!" she cries.

Zeke's bull dog eyes transform into a concert of weird facial tics, like he's secretly being tased.

OMG! Ew! What is his face doing!

"I'm married." I duck down. "To the pope." I tap Collin on the shoulder. "Collin's available though."

"The pope. That's right." Collin snaps his fingers. "Are you Roman Catholic, Zeke?"

"I sure am!" He slaps his knee. "I gave up crack for Lent."

"You see that, Jess? A devout follower."

"Oh goodie."

"It was on account of my lack of jingle." Zeke pats himself down once more. "Also on account of no jingle, I don't have a telephone."

"Get her smoke signal then," says Collin.

"It's a giant middle finger." I demonstrate.

"I don't have a fire pit." Zeke looks through the fence into the railroad ditch, like he misplaced a barbecue set down there.

"Oh, the smokestack on the train." Collin mimes a spade going over his shoulder. "Use your coal car and shovel it into the steam engine."

"Still a middle finger," I say.

"I drive the train." Zeke wags his finger. "The fireman tends to the furnace."

"Well, it's been a sparkling conversation." Collin turns to the fence. "Gotta go."

Leaving Zeke to his own devices, I position Jess on my right and mentally prepare us for the climb.

This fence is friggin' eight feet tall.

And we're off, hooking our claws into the mesh.

We move like it's a three-legged sack race, but with hands and not legs.

Hoisted to the top of the fence, we freeze in two awkward push-ups.

I do not have the upper body strength for this.

In one-two-three, I throw out my leg and saddle the bar.

Alrighty-roo. Here goes nothing. "Wah!"

She misses. She falls. I grab. I anchor, but in doing so, I ramble over the other side.

"Son of a mofo!" *It pinches! It pinches!*

Her body dangles from the rung while mine dangles opposite, two sides of a coin. I latch onto the bar and leap back up there to relieve some of the pain. Zeke is next to Jess at once.

"Collin, help!" She flutter-kicks. "He's hugging me!"

"He's helping you." I can't help but stifle a laugh.

"My name is Gus," says Zeke.

"Collin!"

I dig my feet into the metal holes. "Zeke is helping you."

"I don't want Zeke helping me!"

I shimmy higher so that my chest is pinned over the rail. The air leaves my lungs, but I suffer through long enough to lift my hand from the fence and give Jess enough slack so that she can regrip. Then, out of the blue, comes the last sound I want to hear—a train whistle, screaming twice down the line.

"Nothing to be afraid of," I assure her. "Plenty of clearance between the tracks and the fence."

"Good." I strain my voice. "It means there's clearance on the other side too."

Zeke flares the brim of his hat. "Are you kids hopping the three o'clock to Medina?"

"Ew, no." I squint at him in disgust.

"Come on, Jess," says Collin. "We can be the Boxcar Children."

"We can beat the train," I say.

"Not with me attached to—" Collin glances over my head and does a double take. "Cops behind you!"

Now it's my turn to see a green light where Collin sees a roadblock. It will save my hide and impress his.

"Zeke." I look past my nose. "Boost me over."

The bottom of the bridge gets closer as he pushes me up by the soles. That's when it dawns on me that UP must've seen us through the storm drains in the floor. Before I have time to relay my findings, Zeke shoves me over the top, and I hurdle the bar with too much momentum. My feet hit the dirt with Collin's, quickly followed by our knees. I lift my head from the brush and that's when I see it. On the tracks, through the green, out of the sweltering heat, trundles a big white bullet—yellow handrails, black bumper, red stripes, sixty feet out—moving fast.

"Let's think about this!" Collin shouts, above the clatter. "They'll figure out we got in a fight! People recorded us on their phones!"

"We weren't fighting." I get to my feet. "It was a flash mob for a kick-boxing exhibition."

"I've created a monster."

I wrap my hand around Collin's and rush down the embankment. The white blur is thirty feet out and closing. With my heart beating a drum solo, we leap the rails into the whistling air. Gracefully, I lead with my knee, nimble as an antelope, until my other leg pulls me back. It hyperextends and I collapse to the ground with a thud. Collin jerks back and comes with me. We lay facing each other, eyes like frightened children, which hurriedly shift to the rails. My shoelace is caught on a rivet, my torso in the train's path.

I bury my knees in the grass at Jess's gravesite and arc my back to the sky, entering halfway into what feels like an agonizing yoga pose. Jess always loved yoga. From this position, I remember why I loathed it. I hear something pop and lean forward, my geriatric arms drooped at my side, a .44 Magnum in one hand and a bottle of unpronounceable Russian vodka in the other, both of my mitts aged into rotten prunes. Tears spring out of my craters called eyes and run the crags of my face. *I should've let her hijack that book truck. I should've stopped her from jumping those tracks. What's grand theft auto compared to death by train?*

There was so much I wanted to say. I'll get my chance though. I'll tell her soon. Very soon. I cock the hammer. She's here with me now. I can feel her near—a touch on the shoulder.

I turn my shrunken head up to her angelic form.

"Jess?"

She stands beside me; so young, so beautiful. She hasn't aged a day from the accident. She speaks.

"I'm Lucia. Why are you visiting Great Great Grandma Fisher's headstone with booze and a gun?"

"Ya-You're not dead," I mumble in awe. "How?"

"Um, good genes. I'm 21 years old and don't do drugs. IDK. But we've been looking for you everywhere."

"You're a she-ghost. An apparition!" I hug her by the legs

and cling for solid life. "How I've missed you." I blink hard. "Am I dreaming? Were you in cryogenic sleep?"

An elderly woman steps swiftly behind her, perched on a cane. "That is our granddaughter, you senile old fool."

"Jess!?" I allow the young lady to help me to the old, surrendering gun and drink. "It's you."

"Of course it's me." Her voice is fine gravel.

"Don't you remember?" I ask. "Fifty-nine years ago. We were handcuffed. You were struck by a train."

"The train?" She smiles, amusedly. "No, dear. You stopped being a whiny bitch and rescued me."

"I did?"

"Yes, and right after that you said"—her wrinkled brown eyes gaze into mine—"I love you."

I scratch my head. "That doesn't sound like me."

"I was in a mutual state of shock."

"Tell me," I beg. "How did I save you?"

She places a liver spotted hand upon my cheek. "Remove my foot from the shoe, Grandpa."

I turn tenderly to Lucia, blood of my blood, and the world clouds over.

Fast and true, Collin grabs my ankle and slides it from the heel of my sneaker. I latch onto his collar, and we fling ourselves off the tracks.

"See you yuppies later!" Zeke calls, as the train plows on, horn blaring.

The wheels thunder by, each compartment ripping a new wind tunnel through our hair. Collin stands me up, hugs me tight, then lets go, I think asking if I'm okay. I can barely make out the words. The train is so loud.

"I…" *Don't want to put myself out there and get rejected again.* "You scared the shit out of me!"

I nod and hug him once more, shaken and numb. "You saved my life!"

Collin Marshall saved my life. He's not such a bad guy after all, when he's not pimping me out to the homeless. Physical life aside, what about my social life? It's still on the chopping block. Who is going to save that?

We have limited time to jump the next fence before the train passes completely and the police are able to cross. I trudge up the soil with my bouncy nerves and attack the obstacle like G.I. Jane would a cargo net.

We clamber up the fence, straddle the rail like a pair of witches on a broom, and spill over the top. My balls readjusting, I brush the dust off my jeans, Jess her shins, and light a fire under it. Sprinting, we keep under the bridge until Brown, where up on the sidewalk, we make a clean break for it across the lawn which separates this building from

McFarlane, a freshman dorm, placed inconveniently between us and Carl.

Collin potters along as I paddle for the backside of the dorm. My fuzzy sock collects grime and grass. It feels super weird with one sneaker on, but whatever. A sneaker to spare my life? *Sold!*

Jess reaches an open window—an increasingly appealing shortcut because the clickety-clack of the train just disappeared.

Strands of Christmas lights cover the ceiling inside the dorm. Towels with beachscapes span the walls, and underneath a fake palm tree, two freshmen snuggle, tongue-deep, on the bed.

I help Jess into the window and onto her butt.

"Emergency inspection!"
The canoodling freshmen spring apart.
"Who the hell are you?" the boy asks.

"Your new RA." I throw a leg over and climb in. "This room is clear."

Jess slaps the door on our way out. "Wear a condom."

As we hustle down the hall, I can hear the young basic girl back in her room say, "Ermergerd, the Herndcerff Cerple. I was at this party last night…"

The hallway is loaded with jabronis-in-training and junior-basics packing up their shit—lamps, clothes, TVs—and wheeling it toward the main entrance in big laundry carts. Today is the start of move-out weekend.

"This dorm was named after Seth MacFarlane, you know," I say, squirming around the corner.

"Was it really?" asks Jess.

"Yup, huge advocate of freshman living quarters at Western New York schools."

"Did he used to go here?"

"Never set foot here a day in his life." I dodge a poster tube. "But huge supporter."

"I mean, if he donated a building." Jess hits the brakes. "Yeah, swell guy."

I spot an unattended cart through the outside window of a girl's vacant dorm room, and barrel in to investigate.

I catch Jess's drift immediately. We need that cart. She slides open the pane, welcoming birdsong and the ticking of skateboard wheels into the room, while I welcome her out of it.

Jess hops to the grass three feet below. She gives me space to land and down I jump. I shut the window as best I can, when a skater casually rolls up to us on his board.

"Why are you guys coming out the window?"

I turn from the building, look at Jess, then to Skaterbroni. "Fire drill."

We ignore his confused reaction and ring around the cart, filled to the brim with blouses, dresses and shoes. Seizing the opportunity, I swap out my surviving pink uptown for two new Pumas. They're a size too large, but they'll make do. As for Collin, he needs a disguise, so I throw him a purple tube top dress.

"Put this on."

I give her a shifty look. "You're joking, right?"

"Collin, I am not getting expelled! We have to work together here, for the common good!"

Comfortable with my sexuality, I grasp onto the front and back of my shirt and Hulk-rip the staples right out. Then, I pitch my tatters into the cart, which Jess sweeps away, as she digs a tunnel into the mound of clothing single-handedly. Off come my pants, my boxers breezy with a newfound tear in the cheek. Ass bare, don't care. I step into this Chinese finger trap of a frock and wriggle it up over my legs, now with some chagrin. When I get it above the nips, I have Jess halt the excavation and zip me at the spine.

Yes, this feels emasculating. No, I don't want to get expelled. Yes, I'm aware purple is not my color. No, I'm not wearing underpants. They're in the cart too, where Jess finds me a pair of white, cat-eye sunglasses and plops them on my head. *Oh great.* She then finds a sun hat and attires me accordingly. The ensemble complete, à la freeball, she climbs into the hole she dug, garments on the grass, and burrows inside.

Nice and settled, I turn around to face the new girl. "Don't you look fabulous." I flick down my wrist.

"Quiet." I half-hide, half-smother her face with clothes. "I'm taking you to the cleaners."

Gripping the cart, I look back and *huh*, Skaterbroni was watching us the whole time, consistently lost.

"Pledging for Delta Sig," I inform him.

"Collin," says Jess. "That's a sorority. Do you even college?"

"Silence, woman!"

Skaterbroni ruffles his dandruff, unconvinced. *Ah well.* I hope that jamoke enjoyed the pageant, because I'm taking this fuck show on the road. I place one foot in front of the other, whistling inconspicuously, and push the cart along the path.

Jess pulls a bedazzled blouse out of the way and holds up a stiletto. "I'm going to maim you."

"Not with those chicken wings."

So quick to defend, so mechanically rude. "You should be

nicer to me. Seriously Collin, the look in your eyes when you saved my life doesn't sync up with this whole attitude you have going on. It's not you."

"It isn't?"

"No, but keep it up. See where it gets you." She drops the shoe. "Single."

"Uh-huh."

"Don't play dumb. You're not a complete ass like Duncan and the rest. My wager is, you just have trouble showing emotion."

"Is that so?"

"Yep. The question is, why?" I pause. "Maybe you *do* care what others think of you."

I look down at my dress and laugh. "Yeah, that's it."

She rubs her chin and croons, "Ohhhhhh."

"Oh?" I push her through the freshman courtyard.

"You care what *I* think of you," she ventures.

"Whatever you say, Sherlock."

"Well, you were right about me caring about my social life, and it nearly got me killed, so I may as well ask. How do you do it?"

"Do what?"

"Ignore what people say," says Jess. "Does it come from having nothing to lose or what?"

"You're serious?"

"I asked, didn't I?"

"Sure, okay, I'll give. It comes from knowing your self-worth. If others hate or talk shit, it means they fail to see what you know you've got, and it's their loss." I glance up to navigate the next sidewalk. "Take the value of your teaching skills for example. If that elementary school you like doesn't want you because of that video, then find someplace else to work. The video sucks, yeah, but it's not a death sentence. Your passion for kids will override all that." I flash my teeth. "You think Grandma Fisher never went buck wild?"

Jess laughs. "I wouldn't put it past her." She smiles. "See, you can be nice. And the world didn't end."

"Shhh," I fan my hand. "Not so loud. We are Bonnie and Clyde, remember?"

I bump his fist. "Ride or die."

She drags the clothing back overhead as I turn onto the main strip. I breathe in the freshness of the trees and the dust and the sun, praying to the patron saint of trannies no one recognizes me. I can't have a woodwork jabroni up and spoil Operation Reach-Around. We're so close now, walking by Edwards Hall where the exam was, almost to Smith.

"It's a scorcher out," calls a familiar voice.

I turn to see who's calling.

We're doomed.

Holy she-EE-e-E-eit. Walluski is striding behind me,

and I just looked his way. His elbow-patched arm swings a leather-bound satchel at his side, and his suede shoes, gold buckles, pick up the pace. Slowly, I rotate my head back the way it came. *I'm deaf. I'm deaf.*

"Blah blah bluu blah," I say, cloying at the air.

Walluski claps me on the shoulder, and I nearly shit myself. "Either Miss Fisher is the most horrible sister in the world for letting you wander handcuffed to a cart dressed like a Pixy Stick, or something is rotten in the state of Denmark."

Don't speak, Collin! I'll think of something!

"Judging from your ability to handle that cart," Walluski continues, "I'm going with the latter."

I keep my gaze fixed square on my 12, not showing any indication I possess all five senses. Then I hear it before I see it—a killer bee. Its buzz dances around my ear like a pair of hair-clippers, and I do all that I fucking humanly can not to swat at it. As if that weren't enough incentive, a police officer approaches at a snail's crawl on my left, making steady eye contact and walk-ing invasively close. It's then that I realize the universe is not my friend today, and begin to guess the order in which these turds will hit my fan called life. If the bee stung me first, that would just solve everything.

Or, I could use the situation to my advantage. I scrunch my face up at the cop and pout. Fearful of a lawsuit for tranny profiling, he passes by in a hurry. That leaves me with Walluski and the bee to contend with, which sounds like a puppet show about a child molester when you stop and think about it.

That bee is going to send him into anaphylactic shock if he doesn't stop moving. I can see it through a peephole in my designer rat's nest. Gathering my courage, I dig myself out in full view of Walluski. Collin not knowing what to do, parks the cart in forfeit. Luckily, with Collin stopped, the bee flies on, to which I give him a thumbs up, before turning to meet my maker.

"I have a confession to make, Professor Walluski." Only my face and arm are visible, as I speak from beyond the grave. "I turned 21 last night, and I did a little celebrating. My friend Britney thought it would be funny to handcuff me to Collin here." I hold up the cuffs as proof. "We woke up late, and there was no time to remove them. I'm sorry I lied."

Walluski has an excellent poker face. He pushes his lips from one side to the other, perhaps mulling over some kind of disciplinary action.

"Before you do anything regrettable," I tell him, "I want to say that, if there's anything I learned in the last few hours, it's that Jess Fisher loves teaching kids." I take off my glasses. "I didn't witness her teach, per se, but I did see her drive—in getting to the exam on time, in standing up for her beliefs. Why, she would jump in front of a moving train, risking life and limb, to be a teacher. I lost my job today. Please. Please don't let Jess lose hers."

Collin, you surprise me. He does care under there. I hope that speech did something. My cheek is getting cold, pressed to the stone, as my neck awaits the blade. What's taking so long?

The corner of Walluski's mouth curves up into a smile, and he breaks into laughter. Me and Collin look nervously at one another. This might be good? Walluski waves his chuckling away with the same gesture he uses to wipe a chalkboard.

"Miss Fisher, Miss Fisher. You may not be my brightest student, but you are my favorite student."

Oh God, did he bang her?

Walluski rests his satchel on the cart. "When I allowed you in, I made the decision that, whether you were lying or not, you had arrived on time by any means necessary, and by that I knew you were committed." He unloops the flap on his bag. "That's the type of dedication this field needs." Looking up and to the side, he adds, "Responsibility is a foreign concept, but you've got spunk."

"So you won't make me repeat the course?" I ask.

Walluski withdraws a test booklet from the fold. "I could tear this exam to shreds." He opens to the first page and takes out his red Bic. "Though, frankly, I can't bear to hear you butcher another literary masterpiece, so let's see how you did." He reads the opening paragraph, flips to the end, and reads the conclusion.

"Aren't you going to—"

I pinch Collin's wrist to stop talking.

Walluski leaves his mark, informing us indiscreetly that, "All the classroom's a stage, and all my students merely players." He reveals the grade, winks and repockets the booklet, a C+. "You know, I was 18 once, before the drinking age was 21. At this very college. You think handcuffs are fun, you should've gone to Spring-In '78. My generation could drink yours under the table." He shoulders his bag. "Good luck in your future endeavors, Miss Fisher. See you at commencement."

Walluski steps lively.

"Thank you!" I beam.

"Thank your brother." Walluski turns, walking backwards. "He sat through a two-hour exam, blind, deaf, and dumb. That takes real dedication." He salutes me and departs.

"Did you hear that, Collin?" I say from cloud nine. "I get to graduate!"

"And if police don't nail us, we might even attend." I put on my cat shades and hide her with a pair of Spanx as another cop saunters by, dodging glances at my gender-fluid appearance.

"I already have my lesson plans picked out and oooh, my dad said he's going to buy me a Mercedes!" she squeals beneath the fabric.

"A car that holds gas? God help us all."

The sidewalk bulges into a quad, and my thighs bulge out

of my dress. I push the cart onto a diagonal path lining us up with Smith's front door. The jabronis have ditched their plaid shirts and downsized to wife beaters, and I have to admit, I'm glad I lost my pants. It's like the weather has the flu around here. Jess has got to be baking.

Sweating my balls off.

I put some oomph into it and don't stop until I bump the cart against the concrete steps of Smith.

"Here," I announce.

Jess emerges from the pile and thrusts a leg out of the buggy. She nearly topples over, so I grab her arm to help her stick the landing.

Woozy, I lug my feet up the stairs in my new kicks. Another door, another building, I peel it open and stumble in, dragging myself across the flagstones of a cozy lobby area.

"You wanna stop for a second?" Collin drops his hand at a bench.

"After we see Carl." I wipe a thin film of sweat from my brow and angle us toward the stairway. "I bet you he's got a super slippery chemical to get our hands out."

"That, or a lightsaber." Collin gets the door. "Sure you don't need a drinking fountain?" he asks, plodding up the first flight to the landing. "Jess?"

I open my mouth to respond. Black spots surround

Collin's head. My free hand comes loose of the rail, and I try to touch them, the spots, or rub my eyes, or something, to make them go away, but nothing works. The ceiling wants me.

I reach out while she falls backwards, ball her top in my fist, and lower her body to the floor by the cotton harness that is her shirt. Avoiding a concussion, her arm hangs limply at my side as dead weight.

"Jess!" Delicately, I bend her left elbow in as I bring mine around to cradle her head. "Wake up, babe. Wake up."

. . . .

I pat her on the cheeks. Nobody's home.

Head slouched, I hold my ear to her mouth and listen, though I take such shallow breaths I can hardly tell what I'm listening for. I try to get a grip, and then I hear it. A quiet exhale whispers in my face, timed perfectly with the fall of her chest. *Thank Jesus of Galilee.* She's only dehydrated. Should've drank more Pedialyte, Jess. *God!*

Voices flow in through the cracks of the double doors at the bottom of the stairwell, intruding on our secrecy. We are not safe here for long. I work out the body mechanics required for transportation, hoop my right elbow around Jess's legs, and scoop her up like a bundle of firewood. Cargo loaded, I face the stairs, and go for it. She's about 110 lbs. *I got this.*

Wuhhh, maybe not. My toe kicks into the step, and I throw

out my same foot in the nick of time. Somewhat recovered, I stumble on up, and somehow manage to cross the blue stripe on the tiles at the top marking the end zone. I spin us around, Jess's arm flailing, and press my back against the push-bar.

At that moment, a door downstairs opens and I make a run for it, teetering through a niche study area into a wood-paneled hall. My eyes toggle from right to left, reading the labels on each plaque. Spectroscopy. IR. Chromatography. What room did Carl say again? 208, I think. There it is. Chem Lab!

I brush my fingers against the handle and use Jess's feet to gain entry.

Carl looks up from a packet of papers and slides back his goggles. "Was there a rumble at the drag show?"

"Quick." I shut the door with a mule kick. "She needs water."

"Bring her to the sink."

Carl scooches past me to lock the door, his hair bouncing around like Einstein's. Then, fast as a photon, he meets me at the sink by the back counter. Amongst an array of beakers and ring stands, he turns a faucet and holds a graduated cylinder under the tap.

I don't get it. Jess should've awoken by now with all that racket. She is a heavy sleeper though. It could be like that time she conked out in Music Listening class during the silent disco unit. Her headset was broken, and she woke up at the end in a puddle of drool.

*knock*knock*knock*

Carl and I whip our heads at each other, then fling oursights on the door.

"My professor's back from lunch," says Carl. "We have to hide her."

"Where, in a test tube?"

"Those cabinets." Carl opens one and shoos us in.

"Dude, we can't fit in there." I point to a rack of lab coats. "We can use those lab coats for blankets."

Carl marches to the rack and rips down an armful. When he turns back, one catches on the hook, and leashes him to the wall. While he's busy chasing his tail over there, I lay Jess down onto one of the black-topped tables. Her feet unwind and my arm stays cushioning her head, as I wait for Carl to make his return trip.

He blasts a chair out of the way by accident and, cursing himself, drapes the coats on top of Jess, creating the semblance of a lumpy tablecloth. Then he takes off my hat and snaps a pair of goggles on my face. Thinking better of it, he tosses my hat back on at the last minute, before going to unlock the door. Frantically, I pick up the beakers on the back counter, away from Jess, and pretend I'm doing science.

The door drifts open. A breathy, female voice perks up.

"Jess, why the hell are you under a pile of coats?"

I whirl around as Carl shuts the door behind some girl with shining blonde hair. *Oh yeah, Britney*. Jess told her to meet us.

"And why are you handcuffed to somebody different?" she asks.

"It's the same guy." I dump the coats off Jess. "She's fainted." I wave Britney and Carl toward me.

Britney runs to Jess, fumbling with the zipper on her purse. "How long ago did this happen?" She removes a black case and unzippers that next.

"Five minutes maybe." I point to the case. "What is that? A Starbucks injection?"

"She's diabetic." Britney pricks Jess's finger and transfers a drop of blood onto a strip. "Call an ambulance."

Carl takes out his cell phone.

"Wait." I grab his arm. "Do we absolutely need to? We're kind of in some shit right now."

"Bigger shit than this?" asks Britney.

"We might get expelled," I say. "She wouldn't want that."

Britney glances up from the beep. The gadget reports 53 mg/dl. She starts tapping her leg.

"Is that a good number?" I ask.

"Low." Britney takes out a needle. "Scary low."

"Make the call." I release Carl and nod at the syringe. "Insulin?"

"Glucagon." Britney pushes the liquid into a vial. "Pull her pants down to her knees."

After a brief hesitation, I unbutton her jeans and slide them down.

Britney draws up the fluid, swabs a patch of skin, and plunges the needle into the meat of Jess's thigh.

"We're in Smith Hall in Room…" Carl bites his tongue.

All eyes fall on Jess.

I hug my jacket to my sides to keep out the night air as I trudge along the snow-laden path from my driveway to my porch, eager to send the sitter home and wait for Collin to arrive so that we can exchange gifts. I turn the key, open the door, and who's in the living room to greet me but Blind Frank, in my arm chair, rocking the baby to sleep. Wait, that's not our little boy. That's a loaf of bread.

"Frank! Where the fuck is the baby!"

"Oh hey, Foxy Lady." He startles. "He's uh, right here." He pokes at the rustic French bread, feels the ridges where it was scored, then frowns crookedly as panic sets in. "I knew he felt a tad crunchy today." He rises and reaches under the bolster. "Smelled awfully of gluten too."

"Frank! It's cuz you're high as shit!"

I charge into the kitchen, place my hand on the oven door, recite a small prayer, and rip it open. *Empty.* Crying erupts. Is that my own tears? Where is that coming from? I turn and see Chunk in a bib at the breakfast table engorging himself over a bread pan. On reflex, I grab the biggest knife out of the block and angle it towards him.

"Chunk! If you ate my baby, you're a fucking goner!" I press the knife to his throat. "Eyes above the neckline, Chunk! Did you eat my baby!?"

"No way, Jose." Chunk leaps up from the table. "I'm sure he's kicking around here somewhere." He backs into the living room. "I'll scope out the den."

I chase Chunk past the fireplace and around the Christmas tree. He picks up the choo-choo off the track and heaves it at my head, missing me by a margin, where it instead penetrates the china cabinet, firework-ing with a giant crash of glass. The doorbell rings.

"Pizza's here," says Frank.

He swings his cane at the Douglas fir, picking off heirloom ornaments, during his voyage across the rug. After locating a knob, he opens the door to the grandfather clock, throws in some cash, and pulls out the pendulum.

"I didn't eat a baby," Chunk explains. "It was only garlic bread for the pizza." He lunges for the door.

From through the doorway, out on the porch, Tar Heel adjusts his snapback and marvels at the wreckage. "Hot damn! What have y'alls done to yo house?"

"Oh, you know." I hide the knife. "Some light Yuletide remodeling."

He steps in with the pizza. "Is there a baby crying?"

It's coming from the kitchen, to which I turn and march. On the counter I open the bread box. *Baby Phil!*

I take him in my arms, before another commotion diverts me back into the living room.

Chunk, Javon, and Frank stare at the fireplace. Soot falls from the flue. Soon a voice enters the chamber in song.

"Up on the housetop, click click click HEE-HAW. Down through the chimney with good St. Nick HEE-HAW."

Collin spirits onto the hearth, fat in a red cap sidled by donkey ears. He holds up a bustier on a coat hanger while maniacally revving a dildo attached to a power drill.

Javon drops the pizza. "Oh snap, it's Tranny Claus!"

"He's been translated!" Chunk declares.

"Ho ho ho, who wouldn't go HEE-HAW?"

"No," I say, with glee, and set the baby in his cradle. "It's Saint Nick Bottom." I stroke his beard. "I pray thee, gentle mortal, sing again. Mine ear is much enamour'd of thy note. So is mine eye enthralled to thy shape." I rub his belly. "And thy fair virtue's force perforce doth move me on the first view to say, to swear, I love thee."

Collin whinnies. "Methinks, mistress, you should have

little reason for that. And yet, to say the truth, reason and love keep little company together now-a-days. The more the pity that some honest neighbors will not make them friends." He gestures to our misfit guests. "Nay, I can gleek upon occasion."

"Thou art as wise as thou art beautiful," I coo.

"Not so, neither. But if I had wit enough to get out of this house, I have enough to serve mine own turn."

"Out of this house do not desire to go! Thou shalt remain here whether thou wilt or no. I am a spirit of no common rate. The summer still doth tend upon my state. And I do love thee. Therefore go with me. I'll give thee fairies to attend on thee."

"Who you callin' fairy, lady?" asks Frank, who magically sprouts a pair of wings. So too do Tar Heel and poor Chunk, who cannot sustain flight.

"And they shall fetch thee jewels from the deep," I continue, "and sing while thou on pressèd flowers dost sleep. And I will purge thy mortal grossness so that thou shalt like an airy spirit go—"

"How long does it usually take?" I ask.

"A few seconds," says Britney.

"Water." Carl sets the phone down, scurries to the corner and obtains a bowl of ice. Then he stands next to Jess and dips her hand into the cubes.

"Eek-cold!" I lurch forward.

"She's alive. False alarm." Carl ends a phone call.

The faces around me nod and sigh in relief, and I stop on Britney's. "Britney!" I hold up the cuff. "Why!?"

"Why what?" Britney inspects my wrist. "Oh, my cuffs. It was funny." She sees my rage and contorts her mouth. "It seemed like a good idea at the time."

"I told you I had an a.m. exam!"

"No," says Britney. "You said p.m., distinctly."

I want to tear my hair out.

Britney moves closer to placate me.

"Stay back!" I yell. "You offensive shadow, you canker blossom, you—you bringer of drama!"

"Bringer of drama?" asks Britney, taken aback. "That seems a teensy bit harsh."

Carl checks me for fever. "The fainting must've damaged her prefrontal cortex."

I push Carl's hand off, and look down to see Collin inching my jeans up my legs.

"What are you *doing*?" I hiss, protecting my dignity.

"Not you." He smiles. "You never said you had diabeetis."
I feel my leg. I see my kit. *The glucagon shot.*

"Britney saved your life," says Carl.

"Who are you, again?" Britney asks him.

"I'm the one who held your margarita at the party when you went to use the bathroom." Carl speaks as though he cupped the holy grail for 3.2 seconds.

"Oh, yeaaaah," says Britney. "Hi."

"Thanks Brit." I hop off the table. "BUT, if you didn't

handcuff me to begin with, I wouldn't have needed the stupid shot."

Britney rolls her eyes and spins an imaginary propeller with her hand. "I was going to uncuff you, but I lost the key and you ran off. Whose fault is that?" She parks the propeller on her hip.

"Yours!"

"She's joking," I tell Britney, confidentially. "The handcuffs were a stroke of genius. You deserve a medal. Where'd you get them?"

Britney smiles cheerfully. "Online."

"Great find." I press my thumb to her forehead. "Gold star for you today."

"Um, how about buyer's remorse?" Jess dries her hand on a coat. "I'm pissed."

"If there's someone to be pissed at," I say, "it's Carl." I rap him on the arm. "Nice going with that video, Spielberg. You got me fired."

Carl flips out his hand. "Before or after you woke up late?"

"That wouldn't have made a difference," I say. "Jess's dad runs the place. He would have made up any reason."

"Whelp,"—Carl throws up his hands in dismissal—"I wasn't privy to that intel."

"I said I'll talk to Bruce." Jess places her palm on my shoulder with a glare in Britney's direction. "Once I get my hands free."

"Is the key really gone?" asks Carl.

"With the wind," I say.

"It's in my backpack," says Jess.

"Where's your backpack?" asks Carl.

"The blind guy has it!" says Britney.

"My ex-girlfriend has it," I say.

"Why would the blind guy give your ex-girlfriend Jess's backpack?" asks Britney.

"It's an engagement present," I say.

"To store tampons in," says Jess.

"It was on their registry," I say.

"I love weddinnngs," says Britney.

"Don't we all?" Carl faces the back counter and starts moving his laboratory trinkets around, dillying over here and dallying over there. In a matter of moments, he neatly lays out three bowls filled with ice water, some cloth pads, and a slab of concrete inside of a bin.

I point at the rock. "Are you going to do some sculpting?"

"Nope." Carl stoops to the cupboard and pulls out a shower-caddy-looking-thing with two tanks of God knows what, bearing gauges and valves and Christmas-colored tubes.

"Going to do some cutting," says Carl.

Collin takes off his ridiculous sun hat. "On what?"

"The cuffs." Carl unclips a wand from the carrier. "This acetylene torch should get the job done."

"No way!" I stick our hands behind my back. "I am not letting you come at me with a flamethrower!"

Britney looks at the floor in mourning. "There go the

handcuffs. What will I tell my boyfriend when he wants to play bad cop?"

The nerve of this girl. "Tell him to see me."

Britney rubs her temples. "Why would my boyfriend play bad cop with you?"

"He wouldn't," I say. "I'm going to educate him on the dangers of trusting you with restraint devices."

"Oh yeah?" says Britney. "Maybe I should borrow a new pair when the real cops show up!"

"Are there police in the building?" I ask.

"They will be," says Carl, regretfully. "I called 9-1-1. They know Smith Hall, but not which room. Collin told me to."

"I thought you were dying!" Collin explains.

"I'm not mad, Collin," I say, "just disappointed."

"What!?" Collin cries.

"Kidding." I poke him with my elbow, and turn to Carl and his torch. "Is this our only option?"

"The cuffs are nickel-plated steel, so yes." Carl hands us each a sopping wet rag. "Stuff these into your wrists."

Jess and I do as we're told, pinching the rags between handcuffs and skin.

"Let the chain lay slack." Carl grabs both of our hands and places them onto the concrete altar resting inside of the bin. "When I make the cut, the metal will be over 3,000 degrees Fahrenheit." I flinch at the number, but keep focused on Carl's instruction. "I'll douse the chain, then you two submerge your hands into the bowls of ice water." He eyes us both. "Questions?"

I remain squeamishly silent.

"I thought not," says Carl.

He lowers his welding goggles and grabs a pair of salad tongs. "It might behoove you both to look away."

The igniter scratches out a spark. *Floosh.* The flame kicks on. Carl tinkers with the fuel, fine tuning a brilliant white and blue rod of light, that forces my retinas onto a wall where I study a motivational poster about Achievement and kayaks. There I grind my teeth, heart pounding, my arm stock-still. I can feel the heat radiate off this thing, positive that it's singeing off my body hair. I take a gulp. The torch digresses into a wheeze. Sparks bounce off my fingers like pinpricks. The cut has begun.

Wet rags or not, if Carl aims down the center, which he should, it means that flame is two inches from my skin. Riddled with anxiety, I clear what saliva is left in my throat, and have a hell of a time just doing that.

Then there's Jess.

Britney had slipped a length of gum into my mouth which I now snap and pop, waiting for Carl to cut to the chase.

The hissing retreats, and he turns a knob. "Don't move." He raises his goggles and lays the torch aside.

Red-hot links lay on the block, severed at the points they were initially welded. Carl grabs a bowl and tips it over the chain. A stream of water pours onto the glow in a fast sizzle, the run-off flowing from the block into the bottom of the plastic bin. He then orders us to dunk our hands and gestures to the two remaining ice bowls.

The metal restored to its quieter color, we submerge our bracelets to the rise of steam. That's when it hits me. I can move my arm independently of Collin. I'm unfettered—free. Cue triumphant music! *Haaaallelujah! Haaaallelujah! Hallelujah! Hallelujah! Halaay-heyyy-lu-yah!*

"Jess?" asks Collin.

"I'm good." I snap out of it, my hand going numb. "We need a disguise."

"I second that," I say, looking around. "I left my man-clothes in the cart."

"Lab coats." Carl turns the valves on the tanks. "We'll put them on and leave separately."

Britney hands out the coats.

"What about my black eye?" I ask.

Carl stows the torch back underneath. "Collina's right. She needs a touch-up after her brawl at the gun raffle."

"Collina!" Jess cries, smacking me in the arm, snorting up a laugh. "Collina! Oh my God! Collina! It's funnier the more you say it." She holds her gut and wipes a tear. "But for serious. Collina does need a trip to the powder room."

"You guys are assholes."

I'm reluctant, but it's too late to complain. Jess already has Britney's purse open, digging for makeup. She finds some cream and smears it around my eye.

"A little dab'll do ya," I tell her.

"No, it won't." She continues finger painting.

Carl helps Britney fit her arms through each sleeve of a lab coat, then looks to Jess and says, "Collin has a crush on you."

"Whoa!" I throw my hands out as if stopping two colliding trains.

Jess's gaze travels the short distance from my cheek to my eye.

"Let's all dial it down a gram," I say. "Crush is a little much. It's more like a light squeeze."

What a perfect opportunity.

"I don't know," I say, grinning. "You did have some very kind words for Walluski on my behalf."

"You're doing me a favor with your dad, so I figure I'd do one for you." *Admit nothing! Without reciprocation, she'll have me by the balls. Not on my watch!*

No bueno. He's clammed up again.

"It was very nice, and I bet Walluski thought so too." I resume applying his concealer. "Thank you."

"Got you, babe."

"I think you're lying and I think there's more to it." Jess caps the cream. "However, right now we have a building to evacuate."

"We split up." Carl divvies out the goggles.

"Where should I go?" asks Britney. "I've never been in this building before."

"You spent four years here!" Carl scans the room, astounded. "Really?"

"Hey." Jess puts on her coat. "Neither have I."

"Same." I shake my head.

Carl looks crestfallen. "Your science educations start and stop with Bill Nye. Don't they?"

We all nod in agreement.

Britney pipes up. "Inertia is the property of matterrr."

"You have no idea what that means," Carl says with supreme confidence.

"Yeeese."

"Britney." Carl takes her under his wing. "You go down the main hall and take the stairs into the lobby. That will throw the cops off our scent."

Britney hands Jess her diabeetis medicine, and Britney says, "Text you later, girl," and leaves.

"The lobby will be crawling with cops," Carl predicts. "We're taking the side door."

"Throwing my friend to the wolves, huh?" Jess asks, but before Carl can reply she adds, "Where's the side door?"

"Down this short hallway here." Carl directs her to some point behind the wall. "The stairs lead right outside."

"Perfect." I button my white coat and lower my goggles. "Collin, we'll do this again real soon. Maybe by the ankles next time. I'll let you know about my dad." I pause long enough for him to make a move. *Nothing.* First he's a pushover, now his ego holds him back. *Gawd, so extra.* "Later."

She waves goodbye, gaze lingering, and exits stage left.

I contemplate the rim of my bracelet, now weightless and strangely heavier than ever. Part of me is gone that I never knew I had, while another part of me wishes I had said something. The problem is, she knows where I stand. She knew where I stood four years ago, and she knows where I stand now.

"You know," Carl says, leaning in, "you two would've made a great couple."

"You think so?"

Carl nods, as if sampling a fine wine. "Good chemistry."

"I'll think it over."

"What's to think about? That may have been the last time you'll ever see her."

"We have a date with Frank."

"The blind guy?"

"Yeah."

Carl considers this. "She'll flake."

I take in the information, and suddenly Jess feels more and more unattainable with every step she takes away from this room, the chance passing me by, in a pair of stolen Pumas.

"Doctor Iversen." I straighten my lapels. "If you excuse me, I am late to a symposium."

"Doctor Marshall." He slaps me up front and back and we snap fingers. "Good luck."

"Longest walk of shame of my life," I mutter, stepping out into the hall.

The Chem Lab is situated in the corner of an *L*. I take the short hall, push the door at the end, and find a stairwell made entirely of stone, as if it were carved into a mountainside. The walls, porous and rounded, curve my view gently down the stairs. The door clicks shut behind me as I descend, and I hear a woman's voice below.

"But you are Jessica Karen Fisher?"

"What is this about?" asks Jess.

I stop short, not daring for a second to intervene.

The policewoman speaks so close to me I can count eyelashes. She stands three inches taller, hair in a braid, between me and the side door. The light comes in, reflecting off the grass, the brick, and her badge, summer so near, yet so far. She is Brockport Police, the UP now seeming comparatively insignificant. *Who is to blame? Who ratted me out? Duncan? Alicia? The internet?*

"We impounded a yellow Pontiac Sunfire registered in your name," Lady Cop continues.

"Impounded for what?" I ask.

"Illegal parking, failure to obey a traffic control device, reckless driving, speeding, and unlawfully fleeing a police officer in a motor vehicle."

"Wow, that car did all that?"

Lady Cop leers at me. "Whomever was driving the car did. Officer Leibowitz clocked it on radar this morning."

"I didn't see any Officer Leibowitz."

"Someone pulled out in front of him, and he couldn't pursue."

"Not pursuing me." I smack my hand against my chest. "I wasn't driving."

"You weren't driving your car this morning around 10:50 a.m.? Someone in a Smart Car witnessed you and presumably another student crossing the street nearby your vehicle."

The exam, the fight, the video, the train, the hypoglycemic shock, it all amounts to nothing. Walluski's recommendation is worthless without the degree. I'm as good as expelled. A tear rolls down my cheek.

Lady Cop takes out her handcuffs.

I close my eyes to try to stop the tears.

"I drove this morning."

Who said that? Oh God, it was me!

I amble down the steps and meet the female cop with a pair of surprised eyebrows arching across her face. Hasn't she ever seen a science tranny before?

"And you are?" asks Girl Cop.

I glance at Jess, who looks scared shitless, and turn to the cop. "Collin Marshall," I announce, unwittingly. "I was driving this morning."

"Collin," Jess whispers, "You'll be expelled."

"It was a good run," I say, "while it lasted."

Girl Cop twirls her finger, motioning me to turn. "You have the right to remain silent. Anything you…oh." She finds the cuff. "You brought your own." She gives me a new set. "Have another pair."

She continues the Miranda spiel when Carl scampers down from upstairs. He turns the bend and freezes, adequately bewildered and holding that stupid sun hat.

For a moment, we all stare at each other, then Carl spots my new handcuffs and utters, "Is this because he parked his car in the canal?"

"Oh, that was you?" Girl Cop spins me around. "Were you sober?"

"As a choir boy," I say, eyes big. *They can't prove me wrong now.* "Carl, what the hell? When were you going to say something!?"

Carl takes a few steps down. "I was going to break it to you slowly."

"Car in canal!" I shout. "How do you break that slowly!?"

"First, I begin with a five-minute-long preamble on the construction of the Erie Canal." He places the hat upon my head. "Next, I point out the statutes of New York highway law passed down by the State legislature, and after that—"

Huh, that's why Collin's pants were wet. He must have tried to leave the party to get more beer or something.

"Can we please go now?" I beg the cop.

"Uh, please." Girl Cop grabs me by the arm and leads me through the door.

"Collin!" I cry.

I feel the pressure, the anxiety, all of it, instantly transferred from my life to his. His future is dead so that mine can live. He really cares about me. He really does. But he's not even my type. My type is athletic, tall, dark, and brooding. He has to be a bookworm, and enjoy modern art, and drive a Camaro, and have tattoos, and be a world-traveler, and own a dog bigger than a Scottish Terrier. Oh, and he has to be a Red Sox fan.

"Collin, do you like the Red Sox?"

He cranes his neck around as Lady Cop pushes him out the door. "Fuck no!"

See, not my type. But oh, the feels! Why the feels? Love looks not with the eyes, but with the mind, and therefore is winged Cupid painted blind. *God, the Shakespeare.* Maybe I do have brain damage. But since I'm on the subject, what if Puck's flower juice didn't work and Titania fell in love with Nick Bottom all on her own?

"Be brave, Collin!" I call out the door, and latch onto Carl. "They'll eat him alive dressed like that."

I breathe in the freshly cut lawn and Jess's perfume on my skin as Girl Cop parades me from the sidewalk to the curb, where a squad car awaits me on Monroe Avenue. One of her cop buddies stands dutifully there to receive me while flaunting a smug grin under his mustache. I ignore his delight as he plays chauffeur and opens up the back. Above the flashing lights, I catch sight of a bird-like figure in the courtyard, Professor Higgins, who shakes her head and whittles her fingers with a tsk-tsk motion, the shame-casting bitch!

Then Girl Cop helps me into the car like I'm a toddler more so than a criminal, even going so far as to pat the seat for me. *What service.* She makes sure my hands and legs are inside the vehicle and quietly shuts the door as if putting me to bed.

I try and settle in, despite the discomfort, when the door reopens. For a brief second, I think it's Jess, but no. It's homeless Zeke, of all people! He's being shuffled over from another squad car.

"All aboard." A UP officer places him next to me, and tells Girl Cop, still outside, "We caught him chasing students across the rails again."

Zeke's train hat falls into his lap, and he looks at me like he hadn't just seen me five minutes ago. "I'm Gus."

"Betty," I tell him.

"When I catch them son-um-bitches who sold me out, I'll tar 'n feather 'em good. Tie 'em to the tracks of an inbound lo-comotive, I will."

"Quiet back there," says Girl Cop, climbing behind the wheel. "Exams are in session."

ACT V

Arraignment was fun. Police haven't connected the students in the Sunfire to the ones at the fight on the bridge, so no assault charges, just the rest, unlawful fleeing a cop, etc., which I pled not guilty to. Is there such a thing as lawfully fleeing a police officer? Under what circumstance can you lawfully run from the cops? If they go AWOL and try and kill you? Who writes this stuff? For that matter, why state *unlawful* fleeing? Clearly it's unlawful if it's in the name of a crime. This is the kind of redundant nonsense that passes through my head as I sit in a cold, sticky jail cell with my bail set at a thousand bucks.

The jail warden let me keep the sun hat out of amusement, but really I want it so that Zeke doesn't put two and two together. He hasn't leapt over here from across the cell yet to shank me, so it appears to be working. He just sits and stares, eyeballs googly, with his nose curled in a snarl. His hat they took.

"Why are you in the boys' cage, Buttercup?" Zeke hinges out his arm to acknowledge his cronies, or somebody's cronies—three random guys with holey jeans and full beards who would probably sooner kill Zeke for sport than side with him to kill me.

"It's a co-ed jail." I make no attempt to disguise my voice. "Like the dorms."

Zeke scrutinizes me while gnawing on his tongue with a bicuspid or two. He clearly can't post my bail. I can post his though. His bail is pocket lint and a shirt button. I heard the judge. Bail is set at one button for the smelly crackhead down in front. Remove this yahoo from my presence. *Gavel bang* And yes, Zeke will very well try to reclaim his button after the case is closed. *The State owes me a button, consarn it!*

As for my cool one thousand, it's a toss-up between calling Mom or calling Dad. I promised so much and spoke so big, I honestly don't have the heart to tell either of them. I failed, and failed horribly. Seventeen years of schooling, pissed away for Jess Fisher. Who gets expelled on finals week of college? Love drunk people. That's who.

I spin my broken handcuff around my wrist, going full ADD, while I weave an exit strategy. Yes, the bracelet is still there. The warden had said that U.S. handcuff keys are universal, then left mine on to shame me. The hat wasn't enough, it would seem. He wanted something else to laugh about, and now he's laughed himself to sleep, legs up on the desk, brim low, Barney Fifin' it. Maybe I should wake him. I don't trust these bikers.

The door from the office swings open, distracting me from my worries, so I sit up. In steps a man wearing a suit worth at least five times my bail. The light makes his wavy hair shine and casts a shadow over his gut. He has an athletic frame, and carries both gut and frame proudly over to the desk to give the warden a kick. They must've arrested a mafia don, who they let wander back here unsupervised, to kick awake police staff, by a deal that required a secret pay-off.

"I'm told I inherited a son." The mob boss points me out to the warden. "That's her."

I hyperventilate. It's Bruce Fisher, here to crucify me. The warden sticks the key in the door.

"Hold your horses, Officer Taylor." Bruce holds up his hand to stop. "I'll speak to this pony from his stable."

Thank Lord Jesus.

"Bruce Fisher." He extends his hand between the bars.

I rise from the bench and hesitantly walk to the edge of the cell. *This may not be a smart move.* I extend my hand to introduce myself. "Coll—"

Bruce threads me through the bars and glances down at my torch-cut bracelet. "Jessica's knight in shining armor." He speaks in a frighteningly hushed tone. "I heard what you did for her." His grip is a bear trap. "I hope you can understand. The last thing a father wants to see when he logs into Facebook in the morning—to wish his daughter a happy birthday, mind you— is to see his baby girl in her birthday suit handcuffed to some shmuck."

I swallow hard. "Apology accepted."

"Apology?" Bruce grabs the back of my head. His after- shave, distilled from the holiest of leprechaun piss, wafts out of his pores and onto my taste buds. "I oughta break your legs." He lets that threat pollute the air for a moment and then relaxes his grip. "But you helped my Jessica, so I help you. Here is what is going to happen." He takes me under his wing. "I rehire you as a janitor. You do a good job. You climb up and be a numbers guy. When I say good job, I mean a stellar fucking performance of galactic proportions. Buff the floors. Clean the stains on the break tables. Don't just restock the restrooms." His hand meanders back and forth like a rudder. "I want organic antibacterial hand soap. I want live flowers. Something exotic. You know, like hibiscus or calibrachoa." He prods me in the heart. "I want a fresh spool of double ply shit tickets in my private stall every week!"

He looks me directly in the eye.

"You show up late once, I cut your goddamn balls off and itemize them on my 1120S as a business expense. Are we clear, Miss Marshall?"

"A tax deduction on my castrated testes." I nod. "Got it." I stammer. "Um, there is one small issue though."

"What?" He braces his hip.

"Even if I do perform galactically, I can't become an analyst. I've been charged with a misdemeanor on campus. I'm about to be expelled."

He gives me a sidelong glance. "Do you remember everything they taught you?"

"Most of it."

He releases my neck to jerk off the dust particles. "They can't take it back now."

I take off my hat, relieved I don't need the diploma.

Zeke leaps to his moccasins. "It's you!" He charges at me.

I hold him at bay by his bony collar. "Mr. Fisher. Zeke helped Jess too. He could use a job. Maybe some janitorial work at Laissez-Fare." I look to Zeke. "Plenty of room for vertical mobility." He seems to calm down. "Loads of room. And Jess did say I should be nicer to people."

"I'll give it a think," says Mr. Fisher, sizing up this vagabond. "Pending a thorough background check."

"I stabbed a man in Poughkeepsie once." Zeke stands there slack-jawed. "Will that make my credentials disreputable?"

Bruce glares at me. He lowers his shirt cuffs. "Extremely thorough background check." He snaps at the mini-warden. "Officer Taylor, Mr. Marshall is ready to rejoin society. How much for his homeless sidekick?"

"That'll be…" Officer Taylor checks his clipboard and knocks his hat back. "Gee whiz. Five dollars." He then proceeds to flip through the keys.

"Five dollars?" asks Bruce, confusedly. "Alright, we'll take one of him too."

The warden shrugs and opens up. I dust off my lab coat and step into Bruce Fisher's good graces, with my homeless sidekick moping behind me.

"Your bail money is a thank you gift." Bruce pats me on the chest. "So is my lawyer." We start our way toward the offices when he squints at my face. "Are you wearing concealer?"

"Uh." We pause in the doorway.

"I don't want to know." He marches in like he owns the place. "I assume you need a ride home."

"Unfortunately," I say, in my best professional voice.

"Nice valet work, by the way." He plants me to the floor amidst the cops ferrying paperwork to and fro. "I do hope your little dip in that pig trough occurred before you handcuffed my daughter."

"It did." *I mean, Jess's clothes weren't wet this morning. What did she even say to him?* "Her friend Britney handcuffed us, sir." I set the record straight.

"Is that a fact?" Bruce takes out his wallet and licks his

thumb. "She can just forget about that Mercedes." He tucks a five-dollar bill into the pocket of a passing cop and bounds for the exit. "She's getting a Lexus!"

"How will she survive?" I phrase the question rhetorically, but then in the parking lot Mr. Fisher pivots on his foot and faces me with a stern, hard look in his eye.

"She'll survive by my being there to prevent her from failing."

I sit in a booster seat at the head of the table in the main dining room at the Fisher residence. The place is decorated lavishly. Marble floors, crystal chandeliers, the works. To my left, a row of shots line the table like a bad game of flip cup. Mom captains the team at the opposite end, of which she is the sole member. In front of me is a plate of spinach just out of reach. To my right, Jess crosses her legs in a chair waiting for me to dig in. I stick out my hand once more and stretch, realizing the issue. My hand is a boy's hand. I'm five years old.

Regardless, Mom begins her binge. She cheerses the first shot glass, far away, with an imaginary friend, maybe the devil, clinks it against the table and bottoms up. The glass is placed upside down and up comes the next drink. By the time she reaches me her blood will be fatally poisoned with alcohol.

"Jessy, help." I struggle to reach the spinach. If I get it, maybe I can adult.

"No, I won't spoon-feed you." She smacks her hair in disgust. "I'm not your Mommy."

I turn to Mom, already on her third shot. "Mom, stop! You'll need your stomach pumped!" I turn to Jess. "If you won't help me, help her!"

"No," says Jess, "she has to save herself, like I did."

"Mommy! Feed me and you can go back to drinking! I promise!"

I kick and scream, strapped into this dumb seat. Mom doesn't turn. She doesn't acknowledge. She only keeps drinking, to my neglect.

"She won't feed you either," says Jess. "She was supposed to, but won't, and now it's up to you."

The front door blows off its hinges and men in SWAT uniforms barge in, strapped with battering rams and assault rifles.

"All you grown folk, get the fuck on outta here. Official CPS business," barks the Commander. He walks over and tickles my chin. "Collin, you're coming with us little tyke, where the scary adults can't hurt you."

"You can't take me!" chirps my tinny voice. "I'm a full-grown man!"

"Your inner psyche says different," says the Commander. "Grab him."

The CPS team encircles the table. Jess doesn't move. Mom keeps drinking.

"Wait!" I shout. "Can I at least say goodbye to Mommy?"

The Commander looks at Mom picking up her seventh shot, and then tells me, "Alright, Peter Pan, you have ninety seconds."

Analyze and solve. That's what I'm good at. The objective is spinach. How to execute? My arms are too stubby. I can't pound the table to make the plate bounce closer. I hop, but the chair goes nowhere. Persuading Jess is out of the question. She won't give audience to a boy. This table. It has cracks in it. Lines, interspaced at equal distances. It's a drop-leaf table. I feel beneath the surface for a latch, and there it is. I pull it out and the leaf drops. The plate coasts into my lap. I gobble up the green, hand-to-mouth. *Super Mushroom sound effect* Now I'm a real man.

The CPS team scratch their helmets as I throw out my chair and rush to Mom. I physically pull the ninth shot away from her mouth, but there's no give. Her arm continues upward. I am muscle trying to overpower machine. I barely slow her down.

"You can't save her, Collin," says Jess. "That is not your job." She gets up. "It's hers."

The Commander stands behind my intoxicated mother, assesses my 2.0 version, and barks at his men, "No children here, boys. Just grownup people with grownup problems. Beta team, move out!"

Furious at Mom's behavior, I swipe at the shot glasses on the table and bruise my arm on the rims. The gin, her drink of choice, ripples subtly within their thimbles as the men in combat boots file out the front door. The shots don't budge, as if cemented firmly to the oak paneling. I try to flip the table. It doesn't budge either. Its legs are cemented firmly to the floor. Only Mom can lift the glasses. Only Mom can stop. How did she stop when I was five?

As if in answer to my prayers, Bruce and my dad walk in, just missing CPS.

"Real boujie pad ya got here, Brucey." Dad freezes at the spectacle of Mom firing through a row of shots. "Linda," he roars. "Enough!" The room is silent. "Think of your son."

Mom looks at me. Her eyes frown. She sets her tenth drink back on the table, and keels backwards.

"Maybe that's the problem," I tell Mr. Fisher. "Jess isn't allowed to make her own mistakes."

"Bold talk, Marshall, considering I have your balls in my hands."

"My job you have control over. Jess's life, not so much. She's not a payroll company. Sir," I add, remembering my place.

"Keep talking."

I take a gulp and reveal my analysis. "Your overprotection only pushes her away."

I'm afraid he's about to fire me again, but instead he says, "Okay, Marshall, I'll let that pot simmer." Agitated, he looks up at the clouds, and after a brief communion with his conscience, or somebody, he lowers his chin to say, "I can see why Jess wanted to bail you out." He taps his chest. "It takes a man to stand up to a man."

I smile at the compliment. "Is she here?"

"Over my dead, penniless body." He leads me over to a gleaming Rolls-Royce and opens the back door for Zeke. "What say we go release your companion into the wild?"

"Are you the President?" asks Zeke.

"I know a few handsome bridges he might like," says Bruce.

I scan the car and sigh.

Jess really isn't here.

I unbuckle my seat belt as Britney pulls off along Gordon Street in her gold Camry. She raises the visor, the sun going down, and takes out her cell phone.

"Do you think Collina enjoyed his stint in the slammer?" she asks, a little too peppy.

"No," I retort. "Dad said he had a horrible time."

"Are you sure?" Britney shakes her phone. "I can ask him."

"No no no." I glance at Collin's house. "You stick to the script." I hand her my notes of exactly what to say. "Remember. I'm not with you."

"Then where are you?" she wonders aloud.

"Anywhere but here," I say. "Make the call."

Britney dials my number.

I bring my ear in close. "Does it have any juice left?"

"Shush. Yes, it's ringing."

Meanwhile, back at the ranch…I lay on my bed, arms out, meditating the day's events while the ceiling fan goes round in a circle. Then EDM sounds off from somewhere in the room, rousing me back to consciousness. *What is that?*

Drawn to the music, I carry myself over to the corner by the fish tank, where I peel back a green and gold school hoodie, and unveil a rhinestone-encrusted Android, whose screen reads *Britney-Bear Calling.* I answer.

"Hello, Britney-Bear."

"Collin!" Britney replies. "Where's Jess?"

I smile, hungry with anticipation.

"No clue," says Collin. "It would seem she left her phone in my room."

"Don't move a mole hair. I'll come by and get it," Britney offers.

I give her my address and am about to end the call, but Britney keeps going on and on about her summer plans in New York and Boston and Paris, and I'm not finding a good pause to hang up.

Then, out of nowhere, she says—

"I think Jess likes you. I bet you she's not making a move 'cause you haven't done anything to show any interest."

Here we go.

"Show interest?" he says, with a bit more emotion than he probably wanted. "I just went to jail for the woman."

"Ohhh, so you do like her then?" asks Britney.

"Who wants to know?" He withdraws.

Britney skims the paper for contingency replies.

I shake my head at one line and point to another.

"I do," says Britney. "You can share, you know? My parents say I'm a trustworthy individual. Your secret's super safe with me. I'm graduating with sumo cum loud."

I face-palm.

"Are you visiting Tokyo by any chance?"

"School's over, Collin," says Britney. "What does it matter now?"

I glance down at the handcuff, checked by an alien sense of longing, then cover the receiver. "I've lost my mind." I turn to the fish. "The girl is crazy."

"Not so," says the fish.

"Bah, alright then!" I remove my hand. "Fine. I like her. Are you happy?"

"Am I happy?" Britney asks me.

I nod, feeling superior, and thunderstruck, and blindsided, right in the feels.

"Yes, very happy," says Britney.

I look down at my handcuff and motion for her to mute the call.

"What?" she asks me.

"Do I really want this? How we met, how we hooked up. Everyone will know."

I flick an oatmeal packet against my arm, tear the top and dump it into Roy's bowl. He pokes at the dinosaur eggs with a spoon while I tear another packet for Violet, who pulls her bowl to her chest.

"Mom, I'm too old for dinosaurs." She looks to Collin, up at the breakfast bar on his laptop, going over a client's quarterly budget. "Dad, I'm twelve. Too old, right?"

"Never!" He waves the meal toward him. "I'll take the dinosaurs."

I grab the tea kettle and pour in the hot water. "No time for oatmeal arguments. I'm going to be late for work."

"Surely you can afford a couple minutes," says Collin, "with my sixpence a day salary."

"Wow," says Violet. "That's a lot."

Roy watches the eggs hatch in the water as I pack my students' progress reports into my messenger bag.

"Mommy," asks Roy, "I've been wondering things. How did you and Daddy meet?"

My eyes land on Collin's. "How'd it go again, honey?"

Collin chokes and drops his spoon. "We met uh…listening to music…"

"…while reading Shakespeare plays…"

"…to the blind…"

"…at the homeless shelter…"

"That's right," Collin continues, "now I remember. We took the train there one midsummer, during the Rites of May."

Roy grins at Violet and then looks up at me with his cute little shit-eating cherub face. "That's not what Aunt Britney says."

"The course of true love never did run smooooth." Britney glides her hand toward the horizon.

"Now you hit your cue." I open my door and step out with my pink bag, safely back in my possession. "Keep him talking."

I pace the room littered with soiled clothes and broken dreams.

"Are you sure you don't like, I don't know," asks Britney, "like Alicia instead?"

"In my defense," I say, "it was the first time I had to buy a new car before selling the old one."

What am I saying? Jess? New one? My name's not on the registration, the inspection's way overdue, there's no warranty, I lost the keys, and she drove off on me. At least the airbags look nice. Plenty of space in the trunk too.

"So Jess is an automobile now?" asks Britney.

"Built for speed."

"That's my bestie you're talking about," says Britney.

"School's over, you said. I thought it didn't matter."

"Oh. It matters."

Footsteps in the hall. *Carl?*

"Because," Britney issues a warning, "though she be but little, she is fierce."

The door swings open.

"Ha-haaaa!" I leap in, pointing my lucky pencil. "Gotcha!"

His face is crimson.

"Britney had me on speaker, didn't she?" Collin looks at my bag. "Where'd you stow the body?"

"Alicia's not dead!" I cry. "I didn't even see her. It was Rainbow Dash. She was beckoning to me." I hop Rainbow Dash up and down so I can re-enact how it went using my best Pony voice. "Jess. Jess. Come find me. I'm in the garbage can in Lot A by Britney's car, waiting for gumdrops and kisses. Save meeee! Foolish mortal!"

"I'm sure that's exactly what happened." I note Jess has taken a shower since earlier, swapping her pink top for pink plaid, though she hasn't removed her cuff. "You've changed."

"Yeah." She tugs at her side. "The staples weren't working for me."

"Those clothes should be put in the MoMA."
Jess laughs. "Or in a display case in Drake."

"I had a chat with Bruce," I say. "Thanks for calling in the cavalry."

"I sort of told him we were dating." She bites her lip.

"Oh, did you?" I ask, facetiously.

"Yeah, a final exam is a great first date." She takes a step toward me, taking on a more serious tone. "No guy's ever gone through that much trouble for me before, let alone stood up to my dad."

The door opens behind me. Carl's leaning on the knob, wearing a t-shirt with a Mario PEZ dispenser stamped on its front.

"Clyde," he blurts out in a state of exasperation. "I tried to warn you Bonnie was here. She locked me in the pantry. I survived on nothing but Zebra Cakes and Wheat Thins for forty-five whole seconds." His face recalls the horror. "I was traumatized."

I look at Collin with an impish smile, then turn and deal with Carl.

"That was for the video," I say. "But to show no hard feelings, Britney and I decided to return your science costumes. She's outside with them waiting for you. By the way,"—I grope his chest—"She thinks you're hawt and wants to link up."

"I thought she had a boyfriend," says Carl, verging on orgasm.

"They broke up."

Carl tears down the hall, not a moment to lose.

"Link up-broke up." I tap at my chain link. "I see what you did there."

"You sure about that?" Jess asks.

I smile lopsidedly. "Britney doesn't...want Carl?"

"We'll soon find out." Jess crosses her arms and tosses her hair. "Two can play accidental matchmaker in this town."

"Come here, matchmaker."

Jess sets the pencil on the dresser, slides a single-toothed key from her pocket, and holds it up to the light. She inserts the key into the hole on her cuff. The ratchet slides out. She's free.

"Do me." I hold out my wrist.

"Thought you'd never ask."

The pushover, the pauper, the sales rep, the weaver, the jack-ass, the badass, my partner in crime, I'll take them all.

She loops her bracelet around mine and clasps it shut, linking us together again. *Well, I did say she was crazy.*

His knees cave as I push him onto the bed. Then he takes off my top and flings it across the room with the key.

If she's crazy, so am I.

"If you ever cheat on me…" I bring my lips to his, soft, powerful, and sweet. Then I migrate to his ear lobe to complete my ultimatum. "…I'm going to murder you."
*crash*thud*

Jess and I jump at the shattering of glass downstairs as shards go skittering over the floor of the living room. That would be a brick, sailing through the bay window.

Jess looks down on me, smirky and starry-eyed.

"Isolated incident," I explain.

ACKNOWLEDGMENTS

This book has been a long time coming, having originally drafted it back in 2010 for an intermediate fiction class at Oswego State. It wasn't ready to publish then and neither was I, but, after giving the story a facelift, with my improved writing skills, here we are. I know, so many people to thank for such a short read. What can I say though? You can't rush art.

In reverse chronological order, I want to thank everyone who contributed to IYD, starting with Chrissy and Damonza for bringing the book cover to life. Then, Jake Trask, via Three Fates Editing—thanks for the amazing proofread. You're the man, Jake!

Next, my feedback people. Steve Bauman, you made it through the whole thing. Good on you. Catie Bauman, you made it to page 17. Shame and dishonor to your family. Uncle Joe, you discovered, in your infinite wisdom, that Collin is not in fact riding a *baa-baa* lamb he received from CPS, but is on the lam from CPS. Nice spot. Steph Kula and Angela Marseglia, thank you both for your detailed critiques during winter break. Hwæt! Prof. Ralph Black, thanks for allowing me to submit this to a class which taught me not to be so conventional with form.

Sarah Liu, O Captain! My Captain!..of Three Fates Editing, thank you for the proofread and brilliant line edit. Looking back, I'm glad you hated the story at first. It pushed me to create the dual POVs, one of many changes you came to love. I'm grateful to have you as a friend.

I also want to thank Prof. Jim Whorton and everyone in that prose workshop last fall, including Jim Ryan and McKenna Miller, for providing valuable feedback regarding character arcs, motivations, and POVs.

Now journey with me back in time to 2013. Thanks to Louise Wareham Leonard and to the other students in my Advanced Fiction class at Writers and Books for your comments on characterization. I can't believe I had put this story in third person, past tense. The hell was I thinking?

And before that, came my awesomely bad student film. That's right, a movie. I want to say thank you to Adam Sykut, Danielle Catino, and Drew Whittemore for volunteering to act out my dialogue. Your ad-libs reinspired lines for the characters. Thanks Prof. Josh Adams for the crash course in video editing, David Schuler for letting me use your band's music, Alex Samuel for hosting the premier, and Sophia and Matthew Graves for letting me borrow your house. On the subject of houses and crashing, Drew, thanks for letting me crash for two years, bro.

Prof. Brad Korbesmeyer, a giant thank you for your lessons in screenwriting and for your letter of recommendation to grad school. Exposition! Prof. Patrick Murphy, thanks for offhandedly pointing out the story's connection with Midsummer, and also introducing me to the play. Prof. Mike Slater, thanks for your lectures on the appropriation of Shakespeare's texts in other mediums. Prof. Amy Shore and Prof. Bennet Schaber, thank you for introducing me to the screwball comedy. I must have watched over 30 of them before rewriting IYD for the last time.

Although contributing indirectly, I must thank Prof. Anne Panning and Prof. Steve Fellner at Brockport, Prof. Leigh Wilson at Oswego, and Prof. James McCusker at MCC for nurturing my talent as a writer, specifically with reader orientation, nouns, narrative distance, and simply by showing your own loves of English. Oh, and Prof. McCusker, I totally stole your Jude Law line.

Last but not least, thank you Prof. Bob O' Connor for the literary MPC. In this state I could achieve everything, from using active voice to trimming the excess fat. Thanks to you, and everyone in CRW 306, where it all began, I was able to "go for the jugular".

ABOUT THE AUTHOR

Writer first, bodybuilder second, Paul Bauman was raised on a farm in Western New York and loves and lives in the City of Rochester. He has a BA in Film from SUNY Oswego and is currently attending SUNY Brockport for an MA in English.

A Slytherin by nature, he enjoys people-watching, and narrating their thoughts aloud, as they hurry past him at café tables giving him dirty looks. Other hobbies include comic book nerding, eating Veggie Straws, beach bumming, and not waking up handcuffed to strangers.

www.ingramcontent.com/pod-product-compliance
Lightning Source LLC
Chambersburg PA
CBHW061123100726
47911CB00013B/658